She glared at him in affront. 'You think you can afford *me*, Alessandro?'

His cynical smile cut through her like a scalpel. 'You can name your price, Scarlett. I will pay it to have you in my arms again. And, yes, I can afford you—' his dark gaze raked her mercilessly '—easily.'

Melanie Milburne says: 'I am married to a surgeon, Steve, and have two gorgeous sons, Paul and Phil. I live in Hobart, Tasmania, where I enjoy an active life as a long-distance runner and a nationally ranked top ten Master's swimmer. I also have a Master's Degree in Education, but my children totally turned me off the idea of teaching! When not running or swimming I write, and when I'm not doing all of the above I'm reading. And if someone could invent a way for me to read during a four-kilometre swim I'd be even happier!'

Recent titles by the same author:

INNOCENT WIFE, BABY OF SHAME
ANDROLETTI'S MISTRESS
WILLINGLY BEDDED, FORCIBLY WEDDED
BOUGHT FOR HER BABY
BEDDED AND WEDDED FOR REVENGE
THE VIRGIN'S PRICE
THE SECRET BABY BARGAIN

The Royal House of Niroli:

SURGEON PRINCE, ORDINARY WIFE *(Book 2)*

**Did you know that Melanie also writes for
Medical™ Romance?**

THE SURGEON BOSS'S BRIDE
HER MAN OF HONOUR
IN HER BOSS'S SPECIAL CARE
A DOCTOR BEYOND COMPARE
A SURGEON WORTH WAITING FOR

THE MARCIANO LOVE-CHILD

BY

MELANIE MILBURNE

MILLS & BOON

Pure reading pleasure

First published in Great Britain 2008
Harlequin Mills & Boon Limited,
Eton House, 18-24 Paradise Road, Richmond, Surrey TW9 1SR

© Melanie Milburne 2008

ISBN: 978 0 263 86443 4

Set in Times Roman 10½ on 12¾ pt
01-0708-50273

Printed and bound in Spain
by Litografia Rosés, S.A., Barcelona

THE MARCIANO
LOVE-CHILD

Dedicated to Jocey Anderson, Sue Mayne
and Katrina Henry, three wonderful members
of Talays Aussi Master's Swimming team,
who have bought each and every one of my books
so far. Thank you for being such faithful supporters
both in and out of the pool.
Happy reading and swimming!

CHAPTER ONE

IT HAD started just like any other Monday morning. Scarlett dropped three-year-old Matthew, at crèche after the usual tearful and heart-wrenching 'don't leave me, I miss you too much' routine, before fighting her way through heavy traffic to her small interior-design studio in Woollahra. And just like any other Monday morning her business partner and best friend, Roxanne Hartley, handed her a double-strength latte on her way in the door and asked her how her weekend had been.

'Don't ask,' Scarlett said wearily, and took a reviving sip of the creamy latte.

'So I take it the blind date your sister set up for you wasn't a success?' Roxanne said as she perched on the edge of Scarlett's desk.

Scarlett rolled her eyes expressively. 'Depends what you mean by a blind date. Clearly this guy's idea was to turn up blind *drunk*. He slurred his way through his sob story about his ex-wife for an hour and a half, until I finally managed to escape.'

'Poor you,' Roxanne said in empathy. 'But don't give up yet. There's got to be someone decent out there for you.'

'Decent would be good,' Scarlett said, booting up her

computer. 'A good father-figure for Matthew would be good, too, but as soon as men hear I have a three-year-old son they seem to lose interest.'

'Yes, well, men today can be so shallow,' Roxanne agreed. 'They won't commit, and they want sex on tap.'

'Tell me about it,' Scarlett said as she clicked on her computer mouse to activate the screen to check her list of appointments. She put her glasses on and blinked, once, twice, three times, her heart giving a quick, hard thud when she saw *that* name staring back at her.

'What's wrong?' Roxanne asked in a guileless tone.

Scarlett swivelled her chair to look up at her business partner, her face going pale with shock. 'You made an appointment for *me* to meet with Alessandro Marciano?' she choked.

Roxanne grinned at her excitedly. 'Yes. I wanted it to be a surprise, otherwise I would have called you over the weekend to tell you about it. He phoned on Friday afternoon just after you'd left. It's a huge contract, Scarlett. He's worth zillions, and if we get the deal think of what it will do for us. We'll be featured in every interior-design magazine across the globe. We won't have to pay rent any more, we'll be able to buy the building, no—' She clasped her hands together in glee and added, '—we'll be able to buy the whole street!'

Scarlett sprang to her feet, almost spilling her latte over her keyboard in the process. 'I'm not seeing him,' she said through tight lips. 'I don't want the contract. I want nothing to do with it.'

Roxanne slapped the side of her head as if she couldn't believe what she had just heard. 'Have you happened to look at our financial statements recently?' she asked as she slipped down off the desk. 'Come on, Scarlett, our business loan is stretched to the limit, you know it is. I know things are often a bit slow in January, while everyone is still on summer holidays, but this is a chance in a lifetime. This is just what we need right now. Alessandro Marciano has bought the old Arlington Hotel building in the city. He's going to turn it into a luxury hotel, with three floors of penthouse apartments for the super rich. And he wants us to do the interior design. *Us!* Can you believe it? It's like winning the lottery.'

'I can't see him, Roxanne,' Scarlett insisted. 'Please don't ask it of me.'

A light bulb seemed to come on in Roxanne's head as she peered at Scarlett. 'Hang on a minute, what... Have you dated him in the past or something?'

'More than dated,' Scarlett answered with a dark frown.

Roxanne gave her a probing look. 'What do you mean "more than dated"?'

Scarlett drew in an unsteady breath. 'He's Matthew's father.'

Roxanne's jaw dropped open, and her eyes went saucer-wide. *'He's what?'* she gasped.

Scarlett's expression became rigid with tension. 'I'm not going to see him, Roxanne. No way. I hate him for what he did to me, and I am not going to—'

The unmistakable throaty roar of a Maserati suddenly sounded on the street outside. Both girls looked out of the front window of the studio, and watched as the car's black, sleek body was expertly manoeuvred in between their tiny fuel-efficient vehicles parked outside.

Roxanne met her friend's startled grey-blue gaze. 'Looks like you're not going to have a choice,' she said, and added, with a little sheepish grimace as the front door opened with a cheery tinkle of the bell hanging on the back, 'Er…did I forget to mention the meeting was here, at nine-fifteen?'

Scarlett felt every pore of her skin and every hair on her body stand to attention as that imposing, darkly handsome figure stooped as he came in through the door. Her heart started going like a jackhammer, the pressure building in her chest so overwhelming she wondered if the heavy thumping would be visible through the lightweight white linen of her blouse.

His hazel eyes met hers, the brown-and-green flecks reminding her all over again of the myriad colours of a rainforest. But this time she felt as if there were mysterious shadows lurking in the depths of his gaze, as he stood looking at her in a watchful silence for what seemed like endless seconds.

'Hello, Scarlett,' he finally said in that stomach-tilting velvet drawl that had been her downfall close to four years ago.

Scarlett lifted her chin and turned to Roxanne, who was standing with her mouth opening and closing like a recently landed fish. 'Roxanne, would you please inform Mr…er…' She glanced down at her diary as if to remind herself of his name, before looking back up and continuing in the same haughty tone, '…Mr Marciano that I am not taking on any new clients as I am booked up until the end of the year.'

'But—' Roxanne spluttered, but was cut off by Alessandro who had stepped forward to smile at her with lethal charm.

'Miss Hartley, would you be so kind as to leave Miss Fitzpatrick and I to conduct out meeting in private?' he asked.

'No! Don't you dare leave,' Scarlett bit out hastily. *Please, oh please, don't leave me with him;* she silently begged the rest of the sentence with her eyes.

Roxanne pursed her mouth, and after a moment's hesitation scooped up her bag and half-finished latte. 'Sure, I can do that,' she said, smiling girlishly at Alessandro. 'I have to see a man about some tiles anyway. I'll be back at eleven.'

Scarlett sent her an 'I'm going to kill you for this' glare, before taking her place behind her desk in case her legs followed through on their current threat to fold beneath her.

The studio door opened and closed with another tinkle on Roxanne's exit, but to Scarlett it felt more like the sound of a vault locking down for good.

The silence thrummed in her ears, the air becoming so thick with it she felt as if a pair of hands was around the slim column of her throat, gradually increasing the pressure until she was sure she was going to choke.

'So you are not interested in doing business with me, Scarlett?' Alessandro asked with a coolly impersonal smile.

'No.' Her one-word response came out of her mouth like a hard pellet.

'Why ever not?' he asked with an ironic arch of one dark brow. 'I thought you would be jumping at this chance to get your hands on my money.'

She tightened her mouth even further, and forced her gaze to meet his. 'I am surprised you are interested in engaging the services of a filthy little slut—those were your words for me back then, were they not?'

There was no sign of anger in his expression, but Scarlett could sense it all the same. She had known and loved that face so well in the three months they had been together. Every nuance of it was imprinted indelibly on her brain. The smile that could melt stone, the gaze that could heat blood, the mouth that could kiss like a teasing feather, or with such hungry passion her lips had tingled and been swollen for hours afterwards. Even now, after all this time, she could still taste the salt and musk of his lips and tongue, and her lower body began to pulse with the memory of how if had felt with him plunging between her legs.

She crossed her legs under her desk, fighting the sensations brewing there. But it was almost impossible to control the hit-and-miss beat of her heart every time she encountered that brown-and-green flecked gaze.

'Your sexual proclivities, I would imagine, have no bearing on your talent at interior design,' he said with an enigmatic look. 'You have a good reputation professionally. That is why I am keen to have you wholly responsible for the project I am about to commence.'

Her chin went even higher. 'I told you, I'm not available.'

His mouth tilted slightly. 'Perhaps before you throw away this chance, Scarlett, you should at least look at what I am offering.'

'No amount of money you could dangle in front of me will induce me to conduct any sort of relationship with you again, business or otherwise,' she stated implacably.

A flicker of male interest darkened the brown in his eyes as they moved over her appraisingly. 'I was not going to suggest anything other than a business agreement between us, however…' He left the sentence suspended between them in the pulsing silence.

'Forget it, Alessandro,' she said. 'In any case, I'm already seeing someone.'

'Is it the same man you were involved with in Italy?' he asked, piercing her gaze with his. 'Dylan Kirby was his name, was it not?'

Scarlett felt her blood begin to simmer in her veins. 'I was travelling with him, not sleeping with him.'

Cynicism burned in his gaze. 'Ah, yes, that old story. I remember it well.'

'It's not a story, it's the truth,' she insisted. 'I met Dylan, Joe and Jessica on a bus tour. I told you all this four years ago. How many times do I have to repeat myself?'

'I am not interested in your lies, but I am interested in what you can do for me,' he said. 'Your business is in need of a contract as big as this, Scarlett. You would be a fool to throw it away as if it was worth nothing.'

She clenched her jaw. 'I hate to be the one to point out the irony in all this, but isn't that what you did to me?'

'I am prepared to be generous,' he said, ignoring her comment as if she meant nothing to him.

That was because she *did* mean nothing to him, she reminded herself. He had never spoken to her of love; he had simply enjoyed the delights of their affair while she had fallen in love with him, fallen hard.

Before she had met him she had been a little scathing at the notion of falling in love at first sight, or even of falling in love over a period of days. She had always thought the sort of love that was deep and abiding would build up over a period of time, as trust and respect grew between two people. But meeting Alessandro Marciano that hot summer morning in Milan had tipped her world upside down. Within three hours she had been kissed by him, within three days she had been sleeping with him, and within three months she had been pregnant by him.

Scarlett blinked herself back to the present when Alessandro handed her a document. She took it from him, her shaking fingers not quite able to avoid the fine-sandpaper brush of his against hers. Her whole body jolted in reaction and heat coursed through her, the thud of her pulse going at breakneck speed.

'If you are not happy with that amount, I will double it,' he said.

Scarlett looked down at the contract, her eyes almost popping out of her head at the amount printed there. It was an astonishing amount of money, although she would have to work very hard for it, she imagined. She knew enough about Alessandro Marciano to know he had exacting standards. His reputation as a hotelier was global. Guests staying at a Marciano hotel were treated to the utmost in luxury, and this one in Sydney would be no different, if the drawings his team of highly skilled architects had prepared were anything to go by.

But accepting this contract, as lucrative and career-enhancing as it was, would mean close contact with him, maybe even on a daily basis. There would be meetings with him to discuss her designs, fabrics to look over, light fittings, soft furnishings, plumbing fixtures—the list went on and on in her head. How could she get through it without damaging herself irreparably?

And more to the point how could she keep Matthew safe from knowing his father had refused to accept him as his? Although she couldn't help thinking one look at that child would remove all doubt, even in someone as cynical as Alessandro. They had the same hazel eyes, the same ink-black hair and olive skin, the same-shaped mouth—although Matthew's was still soft with the innocence of childhood.

'I will give you a day or two to think it over.' His deep voice invaded the private torture of her tangled thoughts.

She got to her feet in one abrupt movement. 'I don't need two—'

He held up one and then two long fingers against her mouth. 'Two days, Scarlett,' he said, holding her gaze. 'Think about it.'

Scarlett swallowed as her body remembered how intimately those fingers had known every pleasure spot she possessed. How she had felt that first frisson of passionate response when he had stroked the silken folds of her femininity for the first time—how she had quivered inside and out when he had explored her so thoroughly and so devastatingly with his fingers, his mouth, his tongue, and the hot, pulsing hard length of him.

He lifted his fingers, and she ran her tongue over where he had been, her stomach doing a sudden free-fall when she saw his eyes flick to her mouth.

And stay there.

The air tightened around them, as if an invisible clinging vine had silently insinuated itself into the room and was now pulling them closer and closer together.

Scarlett couldn't breathe; she wasn't game enough to draw in a breath in case he heard the betraying flutter of her pulse beneath her skin.

She stood very still as he reached out again, this time with just the index finger of his right hand, brushing it against the softness of her bottom lip, his eyes still locked on her mouth. The temptation to sweep her tongue over and around his finger was suddenly overwhelming. She had to clamp her teeth together to stop herself taking him in her mouth and sucking on him, as she had done so many times before.

And not just his finger…

His eyes came back to hers, a tiny frown pulling at the dark slashes of his eyebrows, the line of his mouth losing its inherent cynicism for just a brief moment.

'I had forgotten how very soft your mouth is,' he said in an even deeper, more gravelly tone than he'd used before.

Scarlett rolled her lips together, more to stop them buzzing with sensation than to draw his attention back to her mouth— but his eyes dipped again, and this time she felt the heat of his gaze like a brand on her lips.

'I-I think it might be time for you to leave,' she scratched out through her too-tight throat. 'I have nothing further to say to you. I don't want the work. You'll have to find someone else.'

He looked down at her for a long moment. 'I am not quite ready to leave, Scarlett. There are still some things I would like to discuss with you.'

Panic prickled at her insides as she stood stock-still in front of him. She couldn't step back because her desk was in the way, and stepping forward was out of the question, with the possibility of brushing against him to get past.

She was trapped.

'Four years ago you told me you were pregnant,' he said into the silence.

Scarlett felt her throat tighten even further, but somehow she managed to maintain eye contact with him. 'Yes…yes I did.'

'You also told me the child was mine.'

A glitter of anger lit her unblinking gaze. 'Yes, I did.'

'Did you go through with the pregnancy?' he asked after an infinitesimal pause.

She kept her gaze locked on his. 'At the risk of repeating myself—yes, I did.'

His expression remained as unreadable as a book with the pages glued together. 'Does your child have contact with its father?' he asked.

She frowned at him, angry at the way he was crossexamining her. 'What's with all these questions, Alessandro? You were the one who insisted the child couldn't possibly be yours. Why the sudden interest now? Have you suddenly changed your mind and decided I wasn't lying to you after all?'

He gave a little shrug of insouciance. 'No, of course I have not changed my mind. There is no way I could be the father of your child.'

Scarlett sent him a caustic glare. 'So you think.'

'I do not *think*, Scarlett,' he said with a granite-hard stare. 'I know it for a fact.'

She stood before him, silently fuming at his arrogance, her simmering hatred for him threatening to spill over.

His mouth tilted into a sardonic smile as his eyes roved over her lazily. 'Anyway, you do not look as if you have had a child. You are as slim and attractive as you were four years ago.'

She gave him a withering look. 'Thanks for insulting every mother out there who's put on a bit of weight after childbirth.'

'I did not mean to insult other mothers.'

'No, you're here to insult me,' she shot back. 'You can keep your contract, Alessandro Marciano. I don't want anything to do with a man who thinks I am a liar and a cheat and a whore.'

'So even after all this time you are still determined to have me nominated as the sire of your offspring, are you?' he asked with a curl of his lip. 'Why is that, Scarlett—because the other possible candidates would not pay up?'

She ground her teeth as she glared at him. 'There were no other candidates, and you damn well know it.'

The cynicism in the line of his mouth increased. 'You do not like admitting you got it wrong by singling me out, do you,

Scarlett? You thought you had landed yourself a meal ticket for the rest of your life when you met me. I wondered at the time why you had fallen into bed with me so quickly. It all made sense, of course, when you told me your news. You needed financial security, but you got it wrong in selecting me.'

She clenched her fists by her sides. 'I loved you, Alessandro. I *really* loved you. I would have given anything to have spent the rest of my life with you, but not for the reasons you're assuming.'

'Love?' He snorted. 'I wonder if you would still have claimed to love me if I'd told you at the beginning of our affair that I was not interested in having children—ever.'

'Why didn't you?'

Something moved in his gaze, like a shifting shadow. It was there one second, gone the next.

'We had only been seeing each other for three months,' he said. 'I was going to tell you within the next week or two, as I was concerned that you would have hopes for a future of marriage and babies with me. I realise it is a lot to ask of a woman, to relinquish her right to have a child with the man she loves.'

'So you *do* acknowledge that I loved you?'

The cynical slant to his mouth returned. 'I believe you loved the idea of marrying a multi-millionaire. Nothing awakens love so much as money, I have found.'

'Why are you so against having children?' she asked, still frowning. 'I thought all Italians loved children—having a loving family is everything to them, not to mention having an heir.'

'That has never been in my plans,' he said. 'I have other things I want to do with my life. Being tied down with a wife and children holds no appeal at all.'

Scarlett searched his face, wondering what had led him to such an intractable stance, but his expression was inscrutable.

'I will see you in two days' time, Scarlett, to discuss the terms of the contract.' He handed her a card with his business details on it. 'My private phone number is on the other side, if you should wish to contact me before then, otherwise I will see you at the Arlington Hotel on Thursday at ten a.m.'

Scarlett looked down at the gold-embossed card with its serrated edges, the pad of her index finger running over each and every letter of his name. But it wasn't until she heard the tinkle of the tiny bell hanging on the studio door that she realised he had left.

She looked up and watched as he went to his car parked outside, his tall, muscular body almost folding in half to get behind the wheel. He fired the engine and, just before he pulled out into the street, he glanced back and met her gaze, a small frown playing about his brow.

Scarlett turned from the window and drew in a scratchy breath, and held it inside her aching chest until the sound of his car had faded into the distance.

CHAPTER TWO

'I'M WARNING you, Scarlett, that if you don't take this Marciano contract on I'm out of here,' Roxanne threatened early on Thursday morning. 'This is what I've been hoping for ever since I graduated. It's what we've both been waiting for. You can't do this to me— damn it, you can't do it to *us*.'

Scarlett bit her lip, her eyes flicking to the clock again, which seemed to be gathering momentum every time she looked at it. She had less than twenty minutes to get into the city to meet Alessandro and give him her final answer. She had barely slept for the last forty-eight hours, agonising over what to do. Seeing him again had brought everything back, all the heartache and crushing despair of his disbelief and rejection.

'I know you're worried about some of the clauses in the contract,' Roxanne said. 'But we've handled complicated contracts before and sailed through without a hitch. This is an offer too good to pass up. Besides, you know how tight this industry is. If word gets out you turned aside a deal as big as this for personal reasons, how will we hold our heads up professionally?'

Scarlett sank her teeth into her lower lip. 'I know, but…'

'Don't blow this, Scarlett,' Roxanne said. 'If you haven't

signed on the dotted line when you get back to the studio later today, I want you to buy me out of the business.'

Scarlett felt her chest begin to thud with alarm. 'You know I can't afford to do that, Roxanne. It will ruin me. I have no savings, and getting a personal loan would be impossible right now.'

'You've lied to me for close to four years, Scarlett,' Roxanne said bitterly. 'You told me Matthew's father had died in a car accident in Italy. Do you realise how that makes me feel? Totally betrayed. I thought I was your best friend.'

Scarlett met her friend's wounded gaze. 'I know I should have told you, but I was so upset and confused when I came home. It seemed easier to tell everyone Matthew's father had been killed in an accident. I couldn't bear the questions from Mum and Sophie. They would have driven me mad. I wanted to tell you so many times, especially after all you've done for me, but I had to consider Matthew too. How is he going to feel in the future to hear his father wanted nothing to do with him?'

'I realise all that, but what's so hard about taking on several-hundred thousand dollars or more of business?' Roxanne returned. 'Get in the real world, Scarlett. So what if he doesn't believe Matthew's his kid? That's his loss. This is a business transaction. Put your private issues aside and get on with the job.'

'It's not that simple…'

Roxanne gave her a penetrating look. 'You're not still in love with the guy, are you?'

'No, of course not,' Scarlett said with an affronted huff. 'It's just that he's…he's…'

'Very attractive,' Roxanne offered helpfully. 'And super-rich.'

Scarlett glared at her. 'You know I'm not that sort of person, Roxanne.'

Roxanne blew out a breath. 'No, you're not, more's the pity. You're way too kind to people. You let them walk all over you.'

'If you're obliquely referring to the Underwood account, then don't,' Scarlett said with a little scowl. 'I felt sorry for Louise Underwood—her husband was a total brute. I couldn't leave her with all those bills to pay when he ran off with his mistress.'

'We're running a business not a charity, Scarlett,' Roxanne said. 'And, speaking of business, you'd better scoot or you'll never get there in time.'

'I'll get a cab rather than try and park,' Scarlett said as she grabbed her bag and sunglasses. 'God, I wish there was some way out of this.'

'There is,' Roxanne said. 'You sign the contract, you do the work, you say goodbye. Easy.'

Scarlett opened the studio door and grimaced. 'You think.'

When Scarlett arrived at the old Arlington in the city there were various workmen on site, as the building was in the first stages of being gutted. Scaffolding was wrapped around the outside, and the front doors were pinned back to keep them open, but even so the fine dust in the air made her nose start to twitch.

She walked across the threadbare carpet-runner to the reception desk, but she had to step aside as a worn sofa was carried past her to the service lifts. She carried on once the men had moved past, but the reception area was deserted, as the hotel had closed down several weeks ago.

She turned and looked up at the winding staircase and

locked gazes with Alessandro, who was standing on the next floor looking down at her. She felt her stomach fold over itself and her heart start to race as he came down the stairs, the sound of his footsteps echoing throughout the cavernous foyer.

'Hello, Scarlett.'

Scarlett felt the skin on her bare arms lift in goosebumps as he came to stand in front of her. His slightly wavy hair was glossy black with moisture, as if he had not long showered. She could smell the exotic spices of his aftershave, and the clean, male scent of his body, and her brain flooded with images of how he had looked wet and glistening in the shower.

'I was not sure you would come,' he said.

She blinked at him, her mind still back in the shower, her heart beating so quickly she could hear a roaring in her ears. 'Um…I need the money…' she said, but instantly regretted it when she saw the way his eyes hardened slightly. 'I mean, business has been slow over summer, and I don't want to get in too far over my head…or anything…' She bit her lip, hating that she sounded so unprofessional. She was usually so brisk and efficient with potential clients, but Alessandro was not just a client.

He was her little son's father.

Alessandro looked down at her for a lengthy moment. He had spent the last two days thinking about her, wondering what it would be like to have her in his bed again.

This reaction hadn't really surprised him; after all, he had felt the same way the first time he had met her. He could feel it now, the pulse of sexual attraction crackling in the air that separated them. Seeing her again had brought back a rush of memories of how responsive she had been in his arms. He had never experienced anything like it before or since. He felt his groin tightening even now, thinking about the pleasure her body had given him so uninhibitedly. Her slim, golden sun-kissed limbs had snaked around his, her body rocking and shuddering with the spasms of release, until he had exploded with mind-blowing pleasure time and time again.

He was glad now he hadn't told her he had fallen in love with her four years ago—certainly not after the way she had tried to deceive him. That would have been the ultimate in hu-miliation, to have had her know how deeply he had cared for her while she had been cleverly masterminding her plot to hoodwink him.

'So you have decided to work for me after all, Scarlett?' he said into the too-long silence.

Scarlett moistened her mouth with her tongue, her stomach feeling as if a large nest of bush ants had been disturbed inside it. 'Yes… Yes, I have…'

'Because you need the money.'

She swallowed twice before she could find her voice again. 'It's as you said—a big contract. It's also a very time-consum-ing one. I have some other clients that I—'

'Your business partner Roxanne Hartley can see to those while you work for me.'

'This is too big a job to do single-handedly,' she said. 'Roxanne will have to be in on it, as well as one or two other freelance designers.'

'I will leave you to make the necessary arrangements,' he said. 'I am sure you are more than capable of assembling a design team to manage this project.'

'It's not just that.' She took a breath to calm herself and continued. 'I'm concerned about how things are…between us.'

His eyes narrowed ever so slightly. 'What do you mean?'

She hoisted her handbag over her shoulder as she ran the palms of her hands down the sides of her skirt. 'We're not exactly friends, Alessandro.'

'We do not need to be friends in order to get down to business, Scarlett.'

'As long as this remains strictly a business arrangement,' she said with a pointed glance.

His expression contained a hint of mockery. 'Are you saying that for my benefit or your own?'

Her eyes flared. 'What do you mean by that?'

The brown flecks in his eyes darkened to the colour of espresso coffee. 'You can still feel it, can't you, Scarlett?' he said in a low, sexy drawl. 'You can feel that throbbing tension that fills the air as soon as we are in the same room together. I felt it the other day, and I know you did too.'

'That's complete and utter nonsense,' she said with a little toss of her head. 'Anyway, I told you, I'm seeing someone.'

'What is his name?'

Scarlett stared at him, her mind going completely blank. 'Umm…I'd rather not say.'

'How long have you been involved with him?' he asked, still pinning her with his gaze.

Scarlett pursed her mouth and glared at him irritably. 'I thought I was here to discuss the refurbishment of this building, not the details of my personal life. Now, can we get on with it, please? I have a full list of appointments, and I have to pick up my son at five-thirty.'

He held her gaze for a pulsing moment, but she couldn't decide what was going on behind the screen of his hazel eyes.

'Excuse me,' he said as his mobile started to ring.

Scarlett watched as he looked at the caller ID and frowned as he moved a few metres away. It gave her a chance to observe him while he wasn't watching, but she couldn't help wondering who he was talking to in such rapid-fire Italian, his voice sounding edgy and annoyed.

She drank in the sight of him—the long legs, the flat stomach, and the black silky hairs at his wrists where his shirt cuffs were casually rolled up. He looked every inch the successful and powerful man; the world was at his fingertips, and there was nothing he couldn't do if he put his mind to it.

Except acknowledge his son as his own.

Scarlett hated recalling the night she had told him about her pregnancy. She shrank back from the memories, but they marched right through her paltry blockade as they had done so many times before…

'Alessandro, I have something to tell you,' she had said as soon as he had come in from his office in Milan.

He'd placed his briefcase on the floor at his feet and leaned down to kiss her lingeringly on the mouth. 'Mmm,' he'd said, lifting his head momentarily. 'You have been eating chocolate again.'

She'd rolled her lips together and tried to smile, but her stomach had felt like it was unravelling. 'I know you're going to be terribly shocked,' she'd said, capturing her lip with her teeth before adding, 'I can't believe it happened myself… I should have been more careful. I know it sounds stupid and naïve but I just didn't realise how easy it was…'

He'd smiled and tipped up her chin with the pad of his fingertip. 'Let me guess. You have run out of credit on your mobile phone, no?'

'No, it's not that…' Her stomach had tilted again at his touch.

'I told you before, *cara*, money is not an issue with me,' he'd said, stroking her cheek with his thumb. 'I was the one who encouraged you to stay on in Milan for a few extra weeks, so it is only fair that I give you an allowance to tide you over.'

'No, I don't want to take money from you, Alessandro,' she'd said. 'I won't do it. I can get a job in a café or something if I run out.'

He frowned with disapproval. 'No, I do not want you working in a hot, crowded café. I like coming home to you fresh and happy to see me.'

'It's not about money,' she said. 'I have some savings from home I can transfer in any case.'

His thumb stopped moving as he held her gaze. 'You do not like the thought of being paid to be my lover?'

She frowned at him. 'Of course I don't like the thought of it. That's positively archaic, Alessandro. People don't do that, or at least not in the circles I move in.'

His expression was still unreadable as he looked into her eyes. 'I want you to be my lover, and I do not mind paying you to stay with me.'

Scarlett felt her breath stall in her chest. 'For…for how long?'

His thumb moved to her bottom lip and grazed it tantalisingly, his eyes holding hers like a magnet. 'How long would you like to stay in Milan?' he asked.

Her heart began thumping irregularly again. 'How long do you want me to stay?' she asked softly.

He kissed the corner of her mouth. 'The way I feel right now, I want you to stay for a long time—a very long time.'

Scarlett let out her breath in a long stream of relief. She had longed to hear him say he loved her, but it was almost as good knowing he wanted her to stay indefinitely.

'Alessandro…' She stepped up on tiptoe and kissed his mouth in a series of hot, passionate little touchdowns of her lips on his. 'I love you. I didn't think it was possible to love someone so much and so quickly, but I do,' she said, gazing up at him rapturously. 'I love being with you. I love it more than anything in the world.'

He smiled again and brought her closer, his hips pressing against hers. 'I know you do, and I enjoy being with you too. Now, *tesore mio*, tell me what you were so intent on telling me when I came in the door. I am all ears—is that how you say it in English, hmm?'

'Yes…yes, it is.' She took a little breath and announced baldly, 'Alessandro, I'm pregnant.'

He released her so abruptly she stumbled, only just managing to right herself because there was a priceless marble statue close by. She faced him, one hand still holding the statue, her stomach feeling like it was going to drop down between her suddenly trembling legs.

His expression was thunderous with anger, his eyes like chips of murky-coloured ice as they locked on hers.

'Vio slut ripugnante!' His words were laced with venom. *'Vio whore ripugnante.'*

Scarlett's eyes went wide with shock; she had been in Italy long enough to recognise a savage curse when she heard one. Although she had expected him to be surprised, and perhaps a little angry, to have him call her such horrible names was so unexpected she stood without speaking or defending herself for far too long.

'You tried to trick me into asking you to marry me,' he went on in the same cold, hard tone. 'You did not just want my money in exchange for a little affair—you wanted everything, did you not?'

'Alessandro—' She choked on a frightened sob. 'Why are you carrying on like this? I thought you cared for me. I—'

She flinched away as he stabbed a finger in the space between them. '*Siete una frode affamata dei soldi deceitful,*' he snarled.

She swallowed against the burning ache in her throat. 'I'm not sure what you're saying. Please, can you speak in English?'

He stepped closer, one of his hands coming down on her wrist like a manacle. 'You are a deceitful, money-hungry cheat,' he translated viciously, his eyes flashing with sparks of brown and green. 'You are a filthy slut, a filthy whore.'

Scarlett pulled against his iron hold. 'Stop it, Alessandro, please, you're hurting me.'

He flung her arm away and glared down at her. 'You are good at this, I will admit that, Scarlett. But then you are rather accurately named, are you not? You are a scarlet woman if ever there was one.'

She stood as frozen as the statue beside her. 'Don't say things like that, Alessandro,' she said, her heart squeezing in pain. 'You know I'm not like that.'

His bark of humourless laughter had an edge of cruelty to it. 'You opened your legs for me within three days of meeting me, but now of course I know why. You were looking for a father for your illegitimate child. You backpackers are all the same, screwing whatever comes along just for the hell of it. You got caught out and had to find a substitute father in a hurry. Who better than me, a knight dressed in Armani?'

Scarlett could scarcely believe what she was hearing. The malevolence in his tone was so foreign to her. She had never seen him lose his temper. He had never spoken to her so coarsely; she wasn't sure how to deal with it, or indeed how to defend herself. It seemed so out of character; it terrified her that the man she had given her heart and soul to had suddenly changed into someone else entirely.

'Get your things and get out of my house,' he bit out. 'I will give you ten minutes to do so.'

The hammer blows of panic inside her head made her vision start to blur. Her mouth was dry, her heart feeling as if it had been backed over by a truck. Her stomach churned with the nausea that had plagued her for days on end, but she fought against it valiantly as she tried to come to grips with what was happening.

She took a couple of deep, calming breaths. 'You don't mean that, Alessandro,' she said, keeping her voice soft and low. 'You know you don't. Darling, what's come over you?'

His eyes blazed as they looked down at her, his lips pulled tight by a rage so intense she instinctively moved back a step.

'You cannot possibly be carrying my child,' he said, with a flinty glare.

She nervously moistened her mouth. 'But of course it's yours, Alessandro. I've only been with you.'

His lips curled back in a sneer. *'Itete trovando!'*

Her chest tightened another painful notch. 'Please speak to me in English, Alessandro. I don't understand you.'

'You are lying!' He shouted the words so loudly they bounced off the walls, the echoes falling like slaps against her ears.

Scarlett was struggling not to cry. 'I'm not lying. I'd only had one lover before you, and that had been over a year before we met. How can you possibly doubt me?'

'You had been travelling for weeks with that Kirby man, but you tossed him aside as soon as you met me, no doubt because his wallet was running a little dry,' he said.

'That's not true! I have never slept with Dylan. I told him

and the others to leave without me, because I wanted to spend more time with you.'

His expression was cold with contempt. 'That was just a very clever act to worm your way into my affections, was it not?'

Her face fell. 'No...*no*. That's not true. How can you say that?'

'I can say it because it is true,' he said. 'You tried to set me up to pay for your bastard child, but there is one thing you miscalculated about me.'

She swallowed the thorny knot in her throat. 'Alessandro, you're not making sense. We've made love hundreds of times, a lot of times without protection. I went on the Pill too late. I thought it would be safe, but it obviously wasn't.'

His sneer turned to a snarl. 'I have heard of such ploys before. The unplanned pregnancy is a handy way of forcing a man into marriage, but these days it is all too easy to prove paternity.'

'I'll have a test done to prove it,' she said with rising despair. 'Then you'll have to believe me.'

His eyes raked over her from head to foot. 'I have all the proof I need. Now get out of my life.'

She looked up at him in stunned shock. 'You surely don't mean to throw me out on the streets at this time of night?'

His face was set in stone. 'It is where you belong, is it not?'

Scarlett opened her mouth to protest, but he had already turned to call one of the household staff, issuing a short, sharp command to have *Signorina* Fitzgerald's belongings packed immediately and brought to the front door.

Once the servant had scurried away, Alessandro turned back to Scarlett with another look of contempt. 'I must congratulate you on your ingenuity,' he said. 'I have been pursued by many women, but no one has ever got close enough for me to invite them to live with me, albeit temporarily.'

A bubble of anger inside Scarlett finally found its way to the surface. 'I was only ever a temporary diversion for you, wasn't I?' she said. 'You were only interested in a summer fling, and for your own convenience asked me to move in with you. You were never going to make things permanent between us.'

'Permanency is not something I have ever or will ever aim for in my relationships,' he said. 'I value my freedom too much.'

'You're going to end up a lonely old man with no one to love you,' she said, her heart sinking as the servant came down the huge staircase, carrying her backpack.

Alessandro gave a scornful sneer and opened the front door as wide as it would go. 'Goodbye, Scarlett.'

She picked up her backpack where the servant had placed it and slung it awkwardly over one shoulder, her eyes now streaming with tears. 'You're going to regret this one day,' she said, her voice breaking over the words. 'I know you will. You will hate yourself for not believing me.'

'The only thing I will regret is allowing you to fool me into thinking you were not like other social-climbing women,' he said. 'Now, get out before I have you thrown out.'

Scarlett stepped down the stairs with only her pride to keep her upright. She walked stiffly towards the wrought-iron gates, her heart splintering into thousands of pieces as she heard the front door of his house click shut with ominous finality behind her.

CHAPTER THREE

SCARLETT HAD to pull herself away from the past when Alessandro came back towards her with his phone clicked shut. 'I am sorry about that,' he said. 'One of my projects in Positano has been giving me some trouble. Now, let me show you around so you can get a feel for the place.'

She walked with him towards the staircase, her stomach feeling as if not only butterflies but bees and wasps were all vying for a landing space inside.

'I would like the foyer and reception area to make a state-ment,' he said as they climbed the stairs. 'Lots of marble—Italian, of course.'

'Of course,' Scarlett said, and tried not to react as his arm brushed against hers as she stood beside him on the first floor and looked down.

She was shocked that such a simple touch could affect her so much. She had thought she was immune to him by now, after what he had done to her. She had hated him for so long, the heat of it smouldering deep inside her, stoked every now and again by another milestone in her little son's life that Alessandro, out of arrogance, would never see. She had wanted to contact him so many times.

She had considered pursuing him legally, by insisting on

a paternity test to clear her name, but she had been frightened of the consequences. What if Alessandro turned out to be like her father, who had always made it so callously clear he had never wanted a second child? Her father's cruel words to her during her childhood had echoed well into her adulthood. She had lived with the stigma of being unwanted all of her life. She couldn't bear for her little son to suffer the same.

Sunlight came in from the dome above their heads and shafted down in golden rays on the floor below. Alessandro's arm brushed against hers again as he pointed to a shadowed area to the left of the reception desk. 'See that corner over there?' he said.

'Umm…yes,' she nodded, her nostrils flaring as the subtle but tantalising tones of his aftershave wafted past her face.

'What could you do to make that brighter and more open?' he asked, turning to look down at her.

Scarlett felt her heart come to a shuddering halt as his eyes met hers. She swallowed against the sudden thickness in her throat, her palms moistening where they were clutching at her handbag strap like a lifeline. 'I'd need to think about it,' she said. 'Lighting is one option, but there are others. For instance, if we choose a lighter colour for the marble it will throw more light everywhere, not just in that corner.'

His eyes were still locked on hers. 'You are good at this, no?'

She ran her tongue over the arid landscape of her lips, feeling self-conscious and terribly exposed. 'I enjoy it,' she said. 'I like the challenge of bringing new life to old interiors.'

He was standing so close Scarlett could hear the in-and-out of his breathing. She had only to take half a step for her body to come into contact with his, from chest to thighs. She sucked in a breath when he lifted his right hand and cupped her cheek, the touch so like a caress it made her whole body shiver in reaction.

'Don't,' she said in a hoarse whisper. 'Please…'

His thumb moved from her cheek to trace over her bottom lip, the movement slow but incredibly sensual. 'I have been thinking about how good we were together four years ago. Do you remember?' he asked softly.

How could she forget? Scarlett thought. Her body still rang with the echoes of the passion he had awakened. She could feel the pulse of it now as her blood charged through her veins. 'No,' she said. 'No, I don't.'

'No you do not remember, or no you do not want to be reminded?' he asked with a slanted smile.

'I'm here to work, Alessandro,' she said with as much assertiveness as she could muster. 'Nothing else.'

His eyes held hers for an interminable pause, before he stepped back from her and reached for a document lying on a table nearby. 'I trust you have had time to read through the contract I gave you?'

'Yes.'

She drew in a breath as he opened the folder and handed it to her. 'It is marked where you need to sign,' he said. 'Take your time.'

Scarlett bit down on her bottom lip as she looked through the folder page by page, her eyes skimming the words she had read, reread and agonised over for the last two days. She would be able to pay off all her debts and put enough money aside to pay for Matthew's education up to high school. There was even enough for her to employ a part-time nanny to take the strain off him being in child care for such long hours while she worked.

'I will give you carte blanche with the budget.' Alessandro's voice carved a deep hole in the silence. 'I want the best that money can buy.'

She looked up from the document to meet his hazel gaze. 'Why me?' she asked. 'Why are you choosing me for such a huge project?'

His expression gave nothing away. 'You are reputed to be one of the best,' he said. 'And I am in the habit of only settling for the best.'

She screwed up her mouth at him. 'That wasn't what you communicated to me four years ago. Back then, I was the lowest of the low.'

He held her pointed glare for several pulsing seconds. 'But you have since made something of yourself, have you not?' he said. 'No doubt I did you a favour by making you sit up and take responsibility for your actions.'

'*A favour?*' she spluttered. 'Do you have any idea what it's been like for me for the last four years?'

'That is neither my fault nor indeed any of my business,' he said, bending down to pick up the folder she had just dropped. He closed it, tucked it under his arm and met her gaze once more. 'I am prepared to pay you well to do this work for me, but if you are having second thoughts I can just as easily use one of your competitors. I have several from which to choose.'

Scarlett's eyes went back to the folder, her heart skipping a beat at the thought of some other design studio having the chance to work a miracle on this building. It was as Roxanne had said: a chance of a lifetime, and something they had both dreamed of since they had qualified as interior decorators.

'Do you want the job or not?' he asked after a lengthy moment.

She took an unsteady breath and put her hand out for the folder. 'I'll take it,' she said, dearly hoping she wasn't going to regret it.

He opened the folder without taking his eyes off hers, and handed his pen to her, clicking it as he did so.

Scarlett felt the warmth of his fingers on the pen as she took it from him and, to disguise her reaction, laid the folder on the table nearby, bent her head and signed all the relevant sections.

She straightened after she had finished and handed it back to him. 'There,' she said matter-of-factly. 'All signed.'

'Now all you have to do is deliver on your promise,' he said with another one of his enigmatic smiles.

'Umm…yes…' she said, shifting her gaze from the mysterious intensity of his.

He stepped back into her personal space and lifted her chin with two long, strong fingers. 'Four years is a long time, is it not, Scarlett?'

Scarlett felt the magnetic pull of his body, the heat of him so close to her reminding her of the intimacy they had shared in the past. 'Yes.' Her voice came out soft and whispery in spite of her attempt to sound emotionally detached. 'Yes, it is…'

'It is too long,' he said, placing his hands on her hips and bringing her body into closer contact with his. 'I have never felt like this with anyone but you. I have had numerous lovers, but not one of them can arouse me with the way you do. You are doing it now—the way you tug at your bottom lip drives me wild.'

Scarlett let go of her lip and swallowed nervously as she tried to ease out of his hold. 'Please let me go.'

He smiled crookedly as his hands subtly tightened on her

hips. 'You probably have no idea how much I want to kiss you right now, to feel your lips respond to mine as they used to do.'

She stood in the circle of his arms, her heart thumping in case he kissed her, and her stomach already twisting and turning with frustration in case he did not.

She held her breath as his head came down, the first touch of his mouth on hers making her body come to instant, throbbing life. Her breasts felt the press of his chest against them, and her thighs the full force of his arousal as it probed her with heart-stopping intimacy.

It was like coming home after a very long absence.

Everything felt so right.

The skating touch of his hands as they moved to her bottom and pulled her harder against him, the thrust of his tongue into the moist cave of her mouth, and the way he made a sound of pleasure at the back of his throat, made her feel as if the last four years hadn't passed.

The heat of his body warmed hers to boiling point, her mouth melting beneath the pressure of his, and her inner core turning to liquid.

His tongue tangled with hers, flicking then stroking until she was clinging to him without reserve. She kissed him back, her hands snaking around his neck to keep him close, her lower body grinding against the heated trajectory of his.

He angled her face with one hand as he deepened the kiss, his other hand going to her breast in a caress that was temptation and torture rolled into one.

Scarlett wanted more.

She wanted his mouth on her, sucking hard and then softly, as he used to do. She wanted to feel the graze of his teeth, to feel his skin on her skin, to taste his essence, to feel him move deep within her in the most intimate union of all.

She wanted to feel the length and strength of him in her hand, to shape him, to feel him tense with pleasure before he exploded with release.

He pulled back just as her hands brushed tentatively against the waistband of his trousers. 'Not here, Scarlett,' he said. 'We are in full view of the workmen. Why don't we go back to my house and finish this properly, hmm?'

The clinical detachment in his tone was all she needed to get her brain back into gear. 'I don't think so, Alessandro,' she said, stepping backwards, disgusted with herself at her lack of self-control. 'I've told you numerous times, I am not interested in revisiting the past with you.'

His mouth tilted sardonically. 'You did not give me that impression when you kissed me just then. What on earth would your current lover say if he saw you clawing at me so lasciviously?'

Scarlett felt as if her shame was emblazoned on every pore of her skin as she stood before him. She had no excuse for her behaviour. She didn't even understand why she had acted in such a disgraceful way when she hated him so vehemently. She hated him for denying the existence of his son. She hated him for coming back into her life just when she thought she had finally put his rejection behind her.

She drew in an uneven breath. 'I'm deeply ashamed of myself,' she said. 'I should have known this wouldn't work.'

His eyes pinned hers. 'You are reneging on the deal?'

She frowned at the steely glint in his gaze. 'I'm not sure what you are getting at. I told you this was to be strictly business between us. I can't do this any other way.'

'If you do not want to carry through on your commitment you will have to pay a severance fee,' he said. 'It is in the contract you just signed.'

Scarlett felt her insides drop alarmingly. Her eyes went to the folder he had placed back on the small table. She had momentarily forgotten about the severance clause. It had been one of two that had worried her, but she had assured herself the money would be worth it. Now she wasn't quite so sure.

He reached for the document and showed her a sentence just above the section where her final signature was written. 'Do you want me to read it out to you?' he asked.

'No,' she said through tight lips, trying not to look at the words printed there. She had practically signed her life and business away. She would have to pay, and pay dearly, to get out of the contract. She was starting to understand now why he had wanted her and only her. He would no doubt make it impossible to work with him so she would have no choice but to want out of the deal. He had used a thick wad of wordy pages to communicate one sure thing: he was going to ruin her.

She brought her eyes back to his and glared at him. 'I suppose you've done this deliberately, haven't you?'

His expression remained as inscrutable as ever. 'If you mean to imply that I have coerced you into working for me, then I think you need to examine the wording of the contract a little more closely,' he said. 'The terms and conditions are all there in plain English, and I gave you plenty of time to read them.'

She ground her teeth. 'I can see how this is going to be run. You want to pick up where you left off four years ago, and the only way you could do it was to lock me into a business deal that will ruin me if I pull the plug. Isn't that taking revenge a little too far?'

'It is not a matter of revenge, Scarlett,' he said evenly. 'About a year or so ago I came to Sydney on business and I visited a colleague who had recently had his penthouse re-decorated. I was very impressed with the work and was in-trigued, on asking, to find out it had been you who had done the design. I thought it would be interesting to meet you again, to see if what we had was still there.'

She flung herself away from him in disgust. 'I can't believe I'm hearing this,' she said. 'You tossed me out of your life as if I was a bit of rubbish, and never once checked up on me to see if I was all right. I could have been mugged or robbed or even murdered that night, for all you cared.'

Alessandro felt a familiar sharp needle of guilt stab at him. He had been so furious that night, he hadn't stopped to think of anything but getting her out of his life. But, after a young female British tourist had been brutally assaulted a year or so ago a few blocks from his house, he'd realised he should have had Scarlett escorted to the nearest bus shelter or train station at the very least. It had been late, and although he lived in a respectable part of the city she very easily could have met with danger, wandering alone at night.

'I hate you for what you did to me back then,' she contin-ued. 'And I hate you for what you're doing to me now.'

'I am sorry,' he said in a gruff tone. 'I should have thought of your safety. It was wrong of me to treat you so appallingly.'

Scarlett turned around to look at him. 'I had your child, Alessandro, your *son*,' she said, her voice catching over the words. 'Haven't you ever wondered about him?'

His face became an unreadable mask. 'No, for I know he is not mine.'

She balled her hands into fists. 'If he was standing here right now you wouldn't be able to say that with the same arrogant certainty. He has your colouring, and the same eyes and hair.'

'I seem to recall your travelling companion had dark hair and eyes too—or have you conveniently forgotten that little detail?'

She eyeballed him determinedly. 'I did *not* sleep with anyone but you the whole time I was in Italy.'

He rolled his eyes and sighed with impatience. 'I am so tired of this conversation.'

'I am tired of you not believing me,' she threw back in frustration. 'Will you at least agree to meet him and see for yourself?'

'I do not need to see him.'

'Which means you don't *want* to see him,' she said with an embittered look.

'Yes, that is right,' he said with a cutting edge to his voice. 'I do not want to be reminded of your duplicity. Even after all this time it sickens me to think of you lying to me like that.'

Scarlett felt like screaming, and stalked over to the balustrade on the landing to get control. She drew in some deep breaths, her chest feeling so constricted she felt as if hundreds of tiny sharp knives were embedded between her shoulder blades, nicking at her every time she tried to breathe.

'I will leave you to look over the rest of the building,' he said into the taut silence. 'You have my contact details if there is anything you need to check with me.'

Scarlett turned to look at him. 'Why do you want me to work for you when you refuse to believe me about your—'

'Do *not* say it again,' he cut her off abruptly. 'I am not the father of your child, and no amount of times you insist to the contrary is going to change that fact.'

'I just want you to meet him to see it for yourself.'

His brows came together over his eyes in a furious frown. 'I am warning you now, if you bring him to this work site at any time I will sever the contract myself. You will be responsible for whatever debt is incurred as a result.'

'You can't do that,' she said, but there was terror wobbling in her voice at the fear that he could.

He gave her a gelid look. 'Go read the fine print, Scarlett,' he said. 'Then tell me what I can and cannot do.'

Scarlett didn't need to, she already knew.

CHAPTER FOUR

'So HOW did it go?' Roxanne asked as soon as Scarlett came into the studio at lunchtime.

Scarlett dropped her handbag to the floor with a little thud. 'I signed the contract,' she said, her tone heavy with resignation.

'Yippee!' Roxanne jumped up and down, sending her riotous bright-red curls bouncing. 'We're going to be famous!'

'Yes, but there are terms.'

'Terms?' Roxanne stilled and frowned at her. 'What terms?'

Scarlett flopped down in her office chair. 'I can't get out of the contract until I complete the job.'

Roxanne blinked at her. 'So?'

'So I am in over my head,' Scarlett said. 'Both of our heads, actually. If for any reason I don't finish the project, I am liable. We both are.'

'But you're going to finish the job, right?'

Scarlett bit her lip. 'What if he makes it impossible for me to do so?'

Roxanne's throat began to move up and down. 'You mean you think he put that clause in there on purpose?'

Scarlett's brow was still heavily furrowed. 'I'm not sure. I can't help thinking he's very cleverly luring me into his orbit. He told me he'd seen some work of mine and really liked it. I think it must have been Tomasso Venetti's in Bellevue Hill. That's the only penthouse I did last year.'

'You did a fabulous job on that place,' Roxanne said. 'No wonder he liked it. You really have a way with old buildings, Scarlett. I'm sure that's why he's asked you to oversee the Arlington.'

'I can't do it without you,' Scarlett said. 'It's a huge project, and I'm starting to suspect the devil will be in the details.'

'We can handle it, Scarlett,' Roxanne reassured her. 'You just have to keep your head when you're around him.'

'That's the whole trouble,' Scarlett confessed, and dropped her head into her hands. 'I can't think straight when I'm anywhere near him.'

'Look, why don't you get your mum or Sophie to babysit Matthew, and we can go out and have a drink to celebrate landing this contract? We need to think positively about this, instead of dwelling on the negatives. We could go to Dylan's in The Rocks. Everyone is raving about the place since we did the makeover for him. It's one of the most popular restaurants down there now. Besides, we haven't seen him since he broke up with Olivia.'

Scarlett dragged her head up out of her hands. 'You're right,' she said. 'I do need to take my mind off the negatives, and seeing Dylan would be nice. I'm probably being paranoid about Alessandro anyway.'

'Did you tell Alessandro about Matthew?' Roxanne asked.

'Yes, but I got the same response. He still refuses to accept the possibility he could be his child.'

Roxanne rolled her lips together, her brow creasing into a frown as she looked at Scarlett.

'You're giving me that look again,' Scarlett said with an irritated scowl.

Roxanne sat bolt upright. 'I'm not doing any such thing.'

'Yes, you are,' Scarlett said. 'I can see it in your eyes. You don't believe me any more than he does.'

'That's not true.'

Scarlett angled her head pointedly.

Roxanne blew out a breath. 'All right,' she said. 'I confess—I did harbour the thought that you might have somehow got it wrong. For a while there I thought you and Dylan might have had a bit of a holiday fling back then, as even now he always seems to prefer your company to mine. But Matthew is a dead ringer for Alessandro, don't you think?'

'I don't think—I know.'

'Have you told your mum yet?'

'No.'

'Don't you think it's time you did?'

Scarlett released a long-winded sigh and reached for the phone. 'I just know what she's going to say.'

'But, darling, how could you have *lied* to me for all these years?' her mother cried. 'I can't believe you didn't trust me enough with the truth.'

'I wanted to avoid this sort of reaction, that's why,' Scarlett said. 'He's not interested in being a father to Matthew.'

'Not interested?' Her mother's voice was sharp with disapproval. 'Why on earth not?'

'Because he doesn't believe Matthew is his.'

There was a short but telling pause.

'Mum?'

'Darling, you can be straight with me, you know,' her mother said. 'I am your mother after all.'

'Of course I'm being straight with you. There's no possibility of Matthew being anyone but Alessandro's son.'

'None at all?'

Scarlett could hear the doubt in her mother's voice, but this time chose to ignore it. 'No, Mum, there's no doubt at all.'

'Well, then.'

'I know what you're thinking.'

'I'm not thinking anything.'

'Yes, you are,' Scarlett said, mentally rolling her eyes. 'You're thinking what you thought when you said goodbye to me at the airport four years ago—that I would fall in love like you did with a totally unsuitable man and ruin my life.' *Which is pretty much what I did do*, she thought ruefully.

Lenore let out a sigh. 'It's just I can't help worrying about you,' she said. 'You're not streetwise like Sophie.'

'You make me sound like a naïve infant.'

'In many ways you are, Scarlett,' Lenore said, her tone softening with maternal concern. 'You are so trusting of people. I think that's why you ended up with a child out of wedlock. You and I are alike in that sense. We think the best of people when they're not worthy of it. You have to toughen up, love. I've had to—I wouldn't have survived if I hadn't.'

Scarlett let out a sigh as she pinched the bridge of her nose. 'I know.'

'Have you told Sophie about this…this horrible man?'

'Alessandro's not a horrible man,' Scarlett said in his defence. 'He's Matthew's father.'

'He doesn't want the role, Scarlett, so there's no point in thrusting it upon him. Some men are like that, your father being a case in point. You'd be better to move on without him, for Matthew's sake.'

Scarlett knew her mother was right, but a part of her—the part where her pride was stored— wanted Alessandro to accept his son as his own. She felt as if she couldn't move forward until he did. It was like a wrinkle in a carpet—it was going to be a tripping point until it was smoothed out.

'I know how hard it's been for you,' Lenore said. 'You were in a terrible state when you came home from Italy.' Her voice broke as she continued. 'I sometimes think if it wasn't for Roxanne's support in getting your business up and running you would have given up all hope and…done something drastic…'

'Mum…'

Her mother sniffed. 'It's true, darling. You were so thin and run down. But we all assumed you were grieving.'

'I was.' *And I still am,* she added silently. 'It felt like a death at the time.'

'Break ups are like that,' Lenore said. 'The only difference in this case is there's still a body to deal with.'

And what a body, Scarlett thought, recalling how Alessandro had felt under the touch of her hands.

'Will you be all right dealing with this man on a day to day basis?'

Scarlett felt her stomach tremble again at the thought. 'I think so.'

'I'm worried about you.'

'I appreciate your concern,' Scarlett said with heartfelt sincerity. 'But I can handle Alessandro Marciano. He's a part of my past—he has nothing to do with my future.'

'He might have more to do with your future if he suddenly

realises he has a son,' Lenore pointed out. 'What if he meets Matthew some time in the future?'

Scarlett pressed her lips together. 'He doesn't want to meet him, and to tell you the truth I'm starting to think he doesn't deserve to, for what he's put me through.'

'It's understandable that you're angry with him,' Lenore said. 'But think how dreadful it would be if you still felt something for him.'

There was another short but loaded silence.

'You don't still care for him, do you, Scarlett?' her mother asked with an anxious edge to her tone.

'No, Mum. I feel nothing but hatred towards Alessandro Marciano,' she said, trying not to think of how his mouth had felt on hers earlier that day. 'I will never forgive him—ever.'

'Why did you agree to take on this project if you loathe him so much?' Lenore asked.

'I've worked for difficult clients before.'

'You will be careful, won't you, love?'

'Mum, stop worrying about me. I know what I'm doing.'

'How much is he paying you?'

'A lot.'

'How much?'

'Enough,' Scarlett answered. 'I'll be able to get into the black with my business loan.'

Lenore sighed. 'I wish I'd been able to help you a bit more, but my welfare payment is hardly enough to live on and—'

'Mum, stop it. We've been through this a hundred times before. I'm twenty-six years old, far too grown up and independent to be taking money off my mother.'

'I know, sweetheart, but Sophie's done so well, I just wish—'

'Mum, this is me you're talking to, not Sophie. I want different things for my life. I would go crazy living like Sophie does. I hate coffee mornings and bridge parties. I don't want or need a rich husband and designer clothes to feel good about myself.'

'I know that, darling, but sometimes I wish you were a bit more established financially,' Lenore said. 'Wouldn't it be nice if you could find a nice man to settle down with, perhaps have another child, a little half-brother or sister for Matthew?'

Scarlett closed her eyes as she fought against the ambivalence of her feelings. She had one child, a perfect little son who was the image of his father. She wasn't ready to think of having another child by another man. The few dates she had been more or less coerced into by her sister had confirmed she wasn't quite ready to move on.

'Scarlett?'

'I'm OK, Mum, really,' Scarlett reassured her. 'It's just been a heck of a day, that's all.'

'Yes, love, of course it has,' Lenore responded. 'It must have been so hard seeing him again.'

'Yes… Yes, it was…'

There was a small silence.

'Scarlett?'

'It's all right, Mum. I'm not in any danger of making the same mistake twice.'

'I know, but history has a habit of repeating itself, as you know from my experience. I took your father back, and while I'm glad I did, because it meant you were born as a result of our brief reconciliation, I wouldn't want to see you get hurt all over again.'

'I'm not going to allow myself to get hurt,' Scarlett said with a confidence she didn't really feel. 'I've grown up in the last four years, Mum. I'm not going to get my heart broken again.'

* * *

A courier arrived mid-morning with the floor plans of the hotel, but there was no accompanying note inside. Scarlett knew it was inconsistent of her to feel so out of sorts, for she was the one who had insisted it was a business deal and nothing else.

She spent the rest of the day worrying that Alessandro would walk in the door of her studio, and yet as she shut her computer down at five p.m. she felt strangely disappointed and aggrieved that he hadn't.

Matthew was tired, but excited when she picked him up from crèche when she told him his granny was going to babysit him that evening.

'I drewed you a picture,' he announced proudly, unrolling the piece of art paper he had in his hands.

Scarlett smiled as she looked at the bright smudges of paint. 'Wow, that's beautiful, darling. What is it?'

'It's a cat like Tinkles, only not dead.'

Scarlett frowned as she thought about how she had handled the recent death of their neighbour's cat. She had couched it in euphemistic terms, but it seemed Matthew had understood it in his own way.

'It's lovely,' she said. 'Can you do one for Mrs West as well? I'm sure she'd love to have a reminder of Tinkles.'

'Can we get a cat?' he asked as they came to the car. 'Or what about a puppy? I'd *love* a puppy.'

'Darling, we live in a flat,' she said. 'It would be cruel to have a kitten or puppy locked up inside all day.'

His little face fell in disappointment. 'But Mrs West had a cat.'

'I know, but Tinkles was very old and used to living inside, and Mrs West was home with him all day so he never got lonely.'

'What about a daddy?' he asked after a moment. 'Can we have one of those?'

Scarlett disguised her shock by concentrating on unlocking the car and settling him into his car seat. 'I'm not sure about that, sweetie.'

'I wish my real one wasn't dead,' he said as he wriggled into the seat and automatically lifted up his arms so she could snap the restraining belt in place. 'What if we prayed to God and asked him to make him come alive again?'

She had to look away from those big hazel eyes. 'I've prayed and prayed, darling, but it's not going to happen.'

'I'm still going to pray,' his little voice piped up from the back seat as she got behind the wheel a few moments later.

Scarlett met his beautiful green-brown gaze in the rear-view mirror and smiled, even though it hurt. 'Let's hope God is listening,' she said, and took the turn towards home.

Dylan saw Scarlett as soon as she came in the door of his restaurant and, smiling broadly, embraced her in a solid hug. 'It's so good to see you, Scarlett. I was thrilled when I looked at the bookings and saw you and Roxanne had booked in for tonight. It's been a few months since I saw you both. My fault more than yours, so don't start apologising. I've been a bit antisocial since Olivia left.'

'I understand,' Scarlett said, returning his hug.

'So how's the business and Roxanne?'

'I'm expecting her any minute,' Scarlett said. 'She's probably having trouble parking. I had to shoehorn my way into the tiniest spot.'

Dylan smiled. 'Let's have a quick drink together while you wait for her,' he suggested, and signalled for the drinks waiter. 'The apprentice chef I have is brilliant, so I can trust him to hold the fort for a few minutes. The dinner crowd hasn't trickled in yet.'

After two glasses of champagne were set down in front of them, he asked, 'How's Matthew?'

'He's good,' she said with a smile. 'Growing up all the time.'

'He's a cute kid,' Dylan said. 'I loved those photos you emailed me a while ago.'

Scarlett wondered if she should say something about Alessandro, when out of the corner of her eye she saw a tall figure stoop slightly as he came into the bar area with an attractive, willowy blonde on his arm.

'What's wrong?' Dylan asked, leaning forward in concern.

Scarlett swallowed the bitter taste of bile in her throat. 'Er…nothing. I just thought I saw someone I knew, that's all.'

Dylan glanced towards the entrance. 'That's Velika Vanovic, the model everyone is talking about. See how popular you've made me?' he said, turning back to smile at Scarlett. 'Every- one famous or high profile wants to come here and enjoy the ambiance.'

'I think I've seen her on a billboard, she's very beautiful…' Scarlett answered feebly, staring at the bubbles in her glass, hoping the knives of jealousy currently attacking her insides would soon disappear.

'The man with her seems vaguely familiar,' Dylan com- mented, frowning slightly. 'I wonder where I've seen him before…. Hey, isn't he that guy you were seeing in Milan?' He swung his gaze back to her in confusion. 'Scarlett, didn't you tell us he was dead?'

She shifted position in the hope that Alessandro wouldn't see her. 'I can explain…'

'Oh look, they're coming this way.'

Scarlett felt her stomach clench as Alessandro and the glamourous model approached.

'Good evening, Scarlett,' Alessandro said, running his gaze over her appraisingly. 'What a coincidence, seeing you here like this.'

Scarlett rose with Dylan from the sofa. 'Yes,' she said. 'It is.'

Dylan offered a hand to Alessandro with a pleasant smile. 'Hello, Alessandro. It's been a long time. What, nearly four years?'

For a moment Scarlett wondered if Alessandro was going to ignore Dylan's outstretched hand, but after what was probably only a nano-second of hesitation he took it and shook it cursorily. 'Yes, something like that,' he said, his eyes flicking towards Scarlett with an inscrutable look. 'Velika, this is Scarlett Fitzpatrick, the interior designer I was telling you about. Scarlett, this is Velika Vanovic.'

'Pleased to meet you,' Scarlett said, and took the other woman's cold, thin hand briefly.

'Likewise,' Velika said in a husky tone, although the chill of her light-brown eyes belied her comment.

'So,' Dylan smiled pleasantly. 'You're here for dinner as well?'

'Yes,' Alessandro said, his gaze shifting to take in the twin glasses of champagne on the coffee table.

Scarlett felt the scorch of Alessandro's gaze as it met hers; she felt as if every layer of her skin was being lasered off by the heat of it. She knew what he was thinking; she could see it in the rigidness of his jaw. In spite of her assurances to the contrary, Alessandro had always been convinced Dylan had designs on her. He had only met him once or twice, as Dylan, Jessica and Joe had been keen to get on with their tour. But

Scarlett knew that finding her here sharing a drink with Dylan was hardly going to convince Alessandro that nothing but platonic friendship bound them to each other.

'I hope you enjoy your evening with us,' Dylan said. 'I'll organise the head waiter to see you to your table, unless you would like a drink in the lounge first?'

'Thank you, but I think we will go straight to our table,' Alessandro said. 'Velika and I have somewhere else to go after dinner.'

To bed, most likely, Scarlett thought with another sickening wave of jealousy.

Alessandro looked down at her as if he could read her thoughts. 'Enjoy your evening, Scarlett.'

'We will,' she answered with a little hitch of her chin.

Dylan waited until Alessandro and his partner were led to their table before he spoke in a low undertone. 'OK, so you have some explaining to do, young lady,' he said in mock reproach. 'That's Matthew's father, isn't it?'

Scarlett gave him a 'please forgive me' look. 'Yes.'

'I can see the likeness, it's absolutely unmistakable,' he said. 'To tell you the truth, I never really did buy that story about Matthew's father dying in a car accident, but I figured you had your reasons so I kept quiet.'

'I'm sorry…I should have told you. Roxanne is still furious with me about it. You and the others had gone to the States by then. By the time you came back home, I couldn't really tell you one thing and everyone else another.'

He took one of her hands in his and gave it a little squeeze. 'So what gives?'

Scarlett could feel her hand shaking beneath the gentle pressure of his. 'He doesn't believe Matthew is his.'

'Hasn't anyone told him about DNA tests?' he remarked

wryly. 'A friend of mine bought one off the internet. All it takes is a quick swab and the results are back in a couple of days. It puts an end to the argument over paternity right then and there.'

'I begged him to have one at the time, but he point-blank refused. By the time I thought about pursuing it legally, I realised he might not be such a good person to have in Matthew's life.'

'Why's that?'

She picked up her glass and watched as the miniature neck-laces of bubbles rose to the surface. 'My father made it a point to remind me whenever he could of how I was unplanned and unwanted. I didn't want to risk Matthew being exposed to the same.'

Dylan gave her a look of concern. 'You still hold a bit of a candle for him, don't you?'

Scarlett met his clear grey eyes. 'No,' she said with steely emphasis. 'I don't think I will ever be able to forgive him for what he's done. Every day I think about how Matthew has missed out on so much. I can't forgive Alessandro for robbing our child of what he should have had.'

'It's upset you, seeing him with that woman, hasn't it?' Dylan said gently.

'Yes,' she said. 'Of course it upset me. He's living the life of the rich playboy while I've been bringing up his son without support.'

'Money isn't everything,' Dylan put in. 'You've given Matthew a much greater gift in loving him.'

'It's not about the money,' Scarlett said on a sigh. 'It's about the emotional support. It means everything to me.'

Roxanne came in at that point, looking flustered. 'I'm *so*

sorry I'm late, but my car broke down, and I—' She pulled up short when she saw Dylan. 'Oh…hi.'

'Hello Roxanne.' Dylan rose and gave her a brief kiss on the cheek. 'How nice to see you again.'

Roxanne's cheeks became pink, and she looked even more flustered. 'Thanks. You too.'

'Well, I'd better leave you girls to get on with your evening,' Dylan said. 'I can see one of my kitchen staff waving at me.'

He gave Scarlett a close hug and kissed her lightly on the mouth before releasing her. 'Take care, Scarlett.'

Scarlett's smile died on her lips when she caught sight of the slow burn of Alessandro's gaze from across the restaurant. A faint shiver scuttled up her spine as she thought of the power she had given him in agreeing to work for him. Any length of time in his presence was going to be dangerous—and not just professionally…

CHAPTER FIVE

'WOULD YOU mind if we do this some other time?' Scarlett asked Roxanne briefly, describing what had occurred earlier.

'Sure,' Roxanne said, slinging her bag over her shoulder. 'The last thing you need is to see that woman draped all over your son's father.'

Scarlett knew Alessandro had had numerous lovers since her, but even so seeing him with the glamorous model had hurt her more than she had expected it to. She hadn't thought it was possible to be affected in such a way, but her stomach was twisting and turning with anguish even now at the thought of him rushing through dinner so he could take that woman back to his hotel with him.

She tugged herself away from where her thoughts were leading. Why should she care what he did? It wasn't as if she still felt anything for him. She hated him with a vengeance, and nothing but nothing was ever going to change that.

'So, what's going on with Dylan and you?' Roxanne asked as they made their way out to where Scarlett's car was parked.

Scarlett glanced at her friend as she pressed the remote-control device. 'What makes you ask that? You know we've always been friends. There's nothing going on.'

Roxanne rolled her eyes. 'Sometimes you can be so naïve,'

she said. 'Dylan was all over you. No wonder Alessandro was giving you the evil eye.'

Scarlett frowned as she strapped on her seatbelt. 'Dylan's still getting over Olivia. He's lonely, that's all.'

'Lonely baloney,' Roxanne said with a cynical look.

'Are you jealous or something?' Scarlett asked.

'Of course not!' Roxanne insisted. 'He's a restaurateur. He works the most ungodly hours. I pity the woman he eventually marries, she'll never see him.'

Scarlett secretly wondered if her friend was being rather too emphatic in her dislike of Dylan. They had never quite hit it off, skirting around each other on the few occasions they had met, like two wary dogs.

'You know, I've been doing some thinking,' Roxanne said a few minutes later as Scarlett wove her way through the city traffic. 'What if Alessandro changes his mind some time in the future?'

Scarlett glanced at her. 'You mean about Matthew?'

'One look at that child is going to make him have some serious doubts about his convictions,' Roxanne pointed out.

Scarlett's hands tightened on the steering wheel, her teeth nibbling at her bottom lip. 'I know.'

'He could make things very difficult for you,' Roxanne said. 'I have a friend whose sister went through a very acrimonious divorce a couple of years back. As a result, their only child has to travel back and forth on access visits to Melbourne every second weekend. If Alessandro Marciano decides he wants his son to spend time with him in Italy, it's going to be tough on you, not to mention little Matthew.'

Scarlett felt her stomach start to clench again in dread. She had been down this road many times as a young child—forced into access visits that had never turned out the way she had hoped.

Roxanne was right.

Alessandro lived in Milan; he was only here to redevelop the old Arlington Hotel. He hadn't indicated any permanent plans to reside here in Sydney. If he did somehow come to the realisation that he had fathered a child, he might insist on regular access, not stopping to think of how it would affect Matthew to be transported like a parcel through the post.

Matthew was in many ways still a baby. He had not long come out of nappies at night, and still had the occasional accident. He was certainly bright and advanced for his age, but a long-haul flight would be out of the question. Unless of course Alessandro insisted she accompany him, which would throw up a whole lot of other problems—the main one being her ongoing attraction to him. She fought against it assiduously, but each time he was in the same room as her she felt every cell in her body swell in awareness, every fibre of her being tingle in remembrance of the passion they had so briefly shared.

'I feel so torn,' she confessed. 'For years I've wanted Alessandro to face the truth about Matthew, but now I'm worried about what might happen if he does.'

'You're still in love with him.'

'How many times do I have to tell you I'm not?' Scarlett asked in frustration. 'I hate the man.'

'Look, Scarlett, I sometimes think I know you better than I know myself,' Roxanne said. 'You still feel something for him, I can tell every time you mention his name. You get a certain look in your eyes.'

Scarlett gave her a withering glance. 'You're imagining it.'

'Am I?'

Scarlett let out another sigh. 'Look, I admit when I saw him at the restaurant tonight with his latest lover I felt physically ill, but that's because he's hurt me more than anyone else I know. Even my father's crappy behaviour is nothing to what Alessandro's done.'

'Listen, Scarlett, you were in love with him four years ago,' Roxanne said. 'It makes sense that you could fall in love with him again. Believe me, it happens.'

'Yes, I know,' Scarlett said. 'I swore I'd never end up like my mother, falling in love with a man who consistently let her down.'

'I hardly think Alessandro Marciano is in the same category of scum as your father,' Roxanne commented wryly. 'You've only seen your father once since you were a young child, and that was when he came to ask you for money. What a creep.'

'Don't remind me,' Scarlett said with a little grimace of distaste.

Roxanne gave her a reassuring smile. 'You'll get through this, Scarlett. I know you will. We're a team, remember?'

'I know…thanks.'

'We'll knock this project over together and then you can get on with your life. Alessandro will be back in Italy before you know it, and you'll never have to think of him again.'

'Yes.' Scarlet began to gnaw at her bottom lip, a frown almost bringing her brows together over her eyes.

'But you will, won't you?' Roxanne said. 'Think of him, I mean.'

Scarlett released her lip and sighed as she looked at her friend. 'I'm trying not to, but it's hard when I have his son as a constant reminder.'

* * *

As soon as Scarlett arrived at the studio the next morning Roxanne handed her the telephone, cupping her hand over the mouthpiece to whisper, 'It's Alessandro. He wants to speak to you.'

Scarlett took the receiver with an unsteady hand and held it to her ear. 'Scarlett Fitzpatrick speaking.'

'That was a very clever trick, Scarlett,' Alessandro drawled. 'Dangling the opposition in front of my nose to make me want you all the more.'

She felt her face growing hot, and was glad he couldn't see it. 'I don't know what you're talking about. Now, did you want me for something or is this simply a nuisance call?'

'I want to see you.'

'So make an appointment like everyone else does,' she clipped back.

'That is exactly what I am doing,' he said. 'I want to see you this evening at my house.'

Scarlett's heart felt as if it had just slammed into a brick wall and bounced off again. 'Your house? You've got a house?'

'Most people do, do they not?' he said, his tone sounding faintly mocking.

'But…but I thought you'd be staying at a hotel, or a serviced apartment or something.'

'I prefer to have my own space,' he said. 'I bought a house before I arrived.'

Scarlett had to peel her dry tongue off the roof of her mouth so she could moisten her lips. 'So…so how long are you expecting to stay in Sydney?' she asked.

'As long as it takes to see to the business I have here.'

'The Arlington Hotel, you mean?'

'That and some other loose ends,' he responded.

Jealousy rose like a bubbling, hot tide of lava inside her. 'I suppose Velika Vanovic is one of those loose ends?' she put in churlishly. 'You'd better be careful, Alessandro, she's been around the block a few times, or so I've heard.'

'I like a woman who is up front about what she wants,' he returned.

'I hate to imply you have little else going for you, but women like Velika Vanovic are after one thing, and one thing only.'

'Yes, I know,' he said. 'Sex, and plenty of it.'

Scarlett clenched her teeth. 'I meant money.'

'Velika is at least open about it, unlike you, who went about it by more devious means.'

She gritted her teeth. 'I did no such thing.'

'I will expect you here at eight p.m. We will have dinner together to discuss your ideas on the project so far,' he said as if she hadn't spoken.

'I'm not having dinner with you,' she said with stiff force. 'I have another commitment.'

'Cancel it.'

Three beats of silence passed.

'I don't usually see clients out of office hours,' she put in guardedly.

'I am sure you will not mind making an exception for me, since we are old acquaintances, hmm?'

'So what we had together has been downgraded to mere acquaintances, has it?' she asked with bitterness sharpening her tone.

'Old friends, then.'

'We were *lovers*, Alessandro Marciano, and as a result you are the father of my child,' she said through tight lips. 'Don't you dare insult me by referring to me as a mere acquaintance.'

'Are you suggesting you wish to be elevated to the role of my mistress?' he asked.

'Of course not!' she spluttered in indignation.

'It can easily be arranged,' he put in smoothly. 'In fact, I have been thinking about it since I ran into you last night with your boyfriend. He seems pleasant enough, but I bet he has not been able to make you writhe and scream the way I did.'

'It's none of your business what I do or who I do it with.'

'And yet you responded to me so delightfully when I kissed you. I had only to touch you and you went up in flames.'

Scarlett knew she had no way to defend herself, but it didn't stop her trying. 'Lots of ex-lovers temporarily revisit the context of their past relationship. It doesn't mean anything.'

'It means you are still attracted to me, in spite of your involvement with another man,' he said.

'You're a fine one to talk,' she shot back. 'If you're so heavily involved with Velika Vanovic what business did you have kissing me?'

'Ah, but that is what I wish to discuss with you this evening,' he said. 'I will send a car for you, so do not think of trying to wriggle your way out of it.'

'Can I bring my son?'

The silence stretched and stretched, until Scarlett seriously wondered if he had hung up on her.

'I do not think a small child should be up at that hour, do you?' he asked. 'If money is an issue I will pay for a baby-sitter.'

Scarlett let another little silence slip past.

'Don't send a car,' she said, on a sigh of resignation. 'I'll make my own way there.'

'I am sending you a car and I expect you to use it,' he said in a tone that brooked no resistance.

She felt her top lip go up in a sneer. 'Is this a late show of concern for my welfare on the streets alone at night?'

There was a tiny almost immeasurable pause.

'Yes, it is, actually,' he said gravely. 'I deeply regret the way I treated you four years ago. It was ungallant and unfeeling of me.'

'It was also totally unjustified.'

There was another small, tense silence before he broke it by saying, 'I will see you this evening. *Ciao*.'

Scarlett let out her breath in a whoosh, and replaced the receiver on its cradle with a little clatter. 'Ooh I hate that man!' she growled.

'Do you need me to babysit?' Roxanne asked.

Scarlett folded her arms and began to pace the studio. 'I'm not going. I swear to God, I'm *not* going.'

'I'll be there at seven-thirty,' Roxanne said. 'That'll give me time to go to my Pilates class first.'

'I can't believe I signed that contract with that stupid clause in it.' Scarlet was still pacing, her expression thunderous. 'I should have known he would want to tighten the screws, so I had no choice but to get involved with him again.'

'Whoa! Back up a bit,' Roxanne said. 'I think I missed something somewhere. What's this about getting involved with him again? Do you mean involved as *involved*?'

Scarlett scowled. 'He implied something along those lines, but I'm not going to stand for it.'

'Are you sure you can resist him?' Roxanne asked with a concerned look. 'He's one hell of a package, Scarlett. If I wasn't so off men at the moment, I'd be tempted myself.'

'I've changed my mind,' Scarlet said, putting up her chin.

'I'll go around to his house tonight and prove to him that I'm not interested. I'll take some sketches and layouts, and keep things formal and businesslike at all times.'

'Yeah…right.'

'What do you mean, "yeah…right"?'

Roxanne didn't answer, but her expression was communication enough.

'You don't think I can do it, do you?' Scarlett said.

'I think you're in very great danger of getting hurt all over again,' Roxanne said. 'History has a habit of re-marking its territory.'

'Repeating itself,' Scarlett corrected. Roxanne was always mixing her metaphors. 'History has a habit of repeating itself, not re-marking its territory.'

'It's kind of the same thing, though, isn't it?' Roxanne said.

Scarlett was glad the front door of the studio was opened by a client at that point, so she didn't have to answer.

CHAPTER SIX

MATTHEW WAS already sound asleep by the time Roxanne arrived, so Scarlett offered her a drink and sat down to chat to her while she waited for the car Alessandro was sending for her to arrive.

At ten minutes to the hour the doorbell rang, but instead of seeing a chauffeur standing there Scarlett came face to face with the tall, commanding figure of Alessandro himself. 'Oh…It's you.'

He cocked one dark brow at her. 'You were expecting someone else?'

'No, but you said you'd send a car for me. I thought it would be a limo driver or…or something.'

'I was not prepared to take the risk that you would refuse to be transported to my house by my driver, or indeed not turn up at all.'

She glowered at him. 'I'm not that much of a coward.'

Alessandro cast his gaze around the small flat, and encountered Roxanne sitting on the sofa with a bemused expression on her face. 'Good evening, Miss Hartley,' he said. 'Are you babysitting for Scarlett?'

'Yes, but don't hurry back,' she said. 'I've brought a good

book, and there's a late-night movie on the TV I've been dying to see.'

Scarlett sent her a 'what do you think you're doing?' glare, but Roxanne deflected it by sending a beaming smile in Alessandro's direction.

'That is indeed very kind of you, but I will not keep Scarlett out too long,' he said. 'I have an early flight to catch in the morning.'

'Milan?' Scarlett couldn't quite remove the trace of hopefulness from her voice.

His eyes collided with hers. 'Melbourne, actually.'

'Another hotel makeover?'

'Yes,' he said. 'But I will make some time for pleasure as well.'

Scarlett wished she hadn't asked. She followed him out to his car with her stomach churning with jealousy all over again, imagining him with yet another glamorous starlet hanging off his arm. She sat stiffly and silently in the passenger seat as he drove the short distance to the exclusive suburb of Double Bay, but her eyes couldn't help but widen when he turned the powerful car into a driveway she was all too familiar with.

She swung her gaze to look at him. 'You knew I redecorated this property, didn't you?' she asked.

'Yes. I like what you have done to the place. That was one of the reasons I thought I would use you for the Arlington makeover.'

Scarlett didn't give him time to come around to her door, but leapt out clutching her portfolio to her chest like a shield. Her brow was furrowed as she followed him into the house, her thoughts going off in all directions like a box of out-of-control fireworks.

'What would you like to drink?' he asked as he led her into

the huge living area she had designed with meticulous attention. 'I have white wine, champagne, and all the usual aperitifs.'

'White wine, thank you…' she said, still trying to get her head around things.

She had spent a lot of time on this house; the makeover had been total, and she had felt so thrilled with the results. It had gone from being a large but tired 1930's house to a luxury mansion with every modern fixture and appliance. The kitchen and walk-in pantry were huge, the living area twice the size of her flat. Each of the six bedrooms had an *en suite* done in Italian marble, and the main bathroom was second to none in terms of opulence. It had been one of the biggest projects she had ever done, and the payment she had received had helped her and Roxanne move out of the cramped office they had rented in the outer suburbs to their current studio in trendy, upmarket Woollahra.

Alessandro walked to where she was standing, and handed her a glass of white wine as he raised his glass in a toast. 'To a successful completion of our contract,' he said.

A little hammer of suspicion was tapping away inside her head as she held his inscrutable look. 'What's going on, Alessandro?' she asked.

'We are having a drink, are we not?'

'I mean about you happening to be the owner of this house,' she said. 'It wasn't just a coincidence, was it?'

He gave her one of his enigmatic smiles. 'I had one of my employees oversee the work. He spoke very highly of your professionalism and meticulous attention to detail.'

'That would be Mr Rossi, wouldn't it?' she asked, her mouth pulled tight. 'So, he was acting for you.'

'I trusted him to see that the house was brought to a satisfactory standard.'

Her fingers tightened around the stem of her glass. 'I hope you're happy with what I've done.'

His eyes glinted. 'Very. The master bedroom in particular is pure sensual indulgence. I can see your touch everywhere.'

Scarlett could feel a blush rising from the soles of her feet to pool in her cheeks. 'I only did what I was asked to do,' she said, with a white-tipped set to her mouth.

'Yes, but you did it with your own personal flair,' he said. 'It is like making love, no? You have moves and touches no one else can even imitate.'

She gripped her glass even tighter, trying not to be pulled into his force field. She could feel the magnetism of his presence: the way his eyes held hers, the way his too-close body radiated its warmth and very male scent, so that her nostrils flared of their own volition to take more of him in.

He put his wine glass down and stepped closer, tipping up her chin with a lazy finger. 'Just like the properties you have designed, you have left your indelible mark on me, Scarlett,' he said softly. 'No one has ever been able to erase it.'

Scarlett could feel herself drowning in the deep green and brown of his eyes, her whole body on high alert. The blood rushed through her veins, her skin prickled, her breasts felt tight, and her stomach began kicking with excitement as he took the glass from her nerveless fingers and set it down right next to his, all without once releasing her gaze.

Her tongue sneaked out to moisten her lips. 'Alessandro... I can't do this.'

His thumb stroked the side of her mouth, close but not quite touching her pulsing lips. 'But you want to, don't you, *cara*? You want to as much as I do.'

She couldn't stop staring at his mouth, her heart going like an out-of-control jackhammer in her chest. 'It...it doesn't make it right,' she said. 'You already have a mistress, and I have—'

His hands came down on her shoulders and held her fast. 'Do not play games with me, Scarlett. I will have what I want, no matter what hurdles or obstacles you put in the way. We have unfinished business between us.'

'Yes, the birth of your son being one of them,' she threw back.

His jaw was set in taut lines. 'Why do you persist with this? I told you, he cannot possibly be mine.'

'There are ways of finding out for sure.'

His fingers tightened momentarily before he released her, using one of his hands to bring back the hair that had fallen forward over his frowning forehead. 'I do not need to find out anything. I know everything I need to know. I saw you with Kirby; there is an easy familiarity between you. Anyone can see you are intimately involved. I am not surprised he is still on the scene. He never really went away, did he? In fact, it would not surprise me if you cooked the whole scheme up between you.'

She looked at him with contempt. *'What?'*

'Money was your motive,' he said, holding her glare with consummate ease. 'Your job was to land yourself a billionaire so you could get your hands on half of the assets and split them with your lover. It has been done before, and no doubt will be done again.'

'Will you agree to have a paternity test done?' she asked, ignoring his insulting summation of her character.

He looked at her in silence for what seemed a very long time, his expression as closed as a clenched fist. 'If that is the only thing that will stop you going on with this nonsense, then yes, I will agree to it.'

Scarlett suddenly felt suspended between relief and worry. What if on finding out the truth he decided he wanted full custody of his son? What if he insisted on Matthew spending up to half a year in Milan? Matthew was generally a secure little boy, but he was still a toddler, and the slightest change in routine would be enough to make him have nightmares or set him back developmentally. She might very well have started a chain of events that, once in motion, would not be easily halted.

Alessandro was a determined and no-nonsense man. Once he found out the truth, he would want control, and she had virtually handed it to him by pressing the issue so persistently.

'We don't have to rush into things…' she said, knowing it sounded as if she was backtracking.

His lip curled. 'Having second thoughts, Scarlett?'

She forced herself to hold his gaze. 'No, but I'm concerned about the effect on my son. I've always told him his father is dead.'

'He is very young to understand the concept of death,' he commented. 'He must be a very intelligent child.'

'He is,' she said, lifting her chin. 'But then, so is his father.'

He picked up their glasses, handing her the one she hadn't yet tasted. 'Dinner is ready,' he said. 'I had my housekeeper prepare it earlier.'

Scarlett followed him to the dining area she had designed for a happy family gathering, never once at the time imagining that a few months later she would be sitting in it in a stony silence, opposite the man who had so ruthlessly broken her heart.

She sat, staring at the food on her plate, wondering how on earth she was going to get it past the aching lump in her throat.

'You are not eating,' Alessandro said after a few moments. 'Is the food not to your liking?'

She picked up her knife and fork. 'It's fine…lovely, in fact. You must have a very good housekeeper.'

'Yes, I have,' he said. 'She only comes in twice a week, however.'

Scarlett looked up in surprise from rearranging the food on her plate. 'Is that all? I thought you'd have a daily, if not full-time help.'

He picked up his wine glass and met her gaze. 'I do not like sharing my living space with people who are virtually strangers. I thought you would have remembered that about me.'

Scarlett did, but she thought with his billionaire status it might have changed. Alessandro had always been very particular about his privacy. She hadn't met any member of his extended family in the whole time she had lived with him. When she had asked about his parents, whether they were coming to visit or if they could visit them, he had told her they were on an extended cruise and wouldn't be back for months. All he had told her was that he was an only child, but now she wondered if there was more to his background than he was prepared to reveal.

'How are your parents?' she asked after a slight pause.

'Fine.'

'Where are they based now?' she asked. 'Do they live in Milan close to you?'

'No, in Sorrento,' he answered. 'They have a nice place overlooking the sea.'

'So you see them often?'

'No.'

'They must miss you,' she offered into the ensuing lengthy silence.

His eyes fell away from hers. 'Yes…' he said, with a slight frown pleating his brow. 'I imagine they do.'

Scarlett picked up her glass and took a tiny sip. 'Will they come out to visit you while you're here in Australia?' she asked.

'They have talked about it once or twice, but nothing has been confirmed.'

'Do you have a photograph of them?' she asked.

His eyes were shadowed as they met hers. 'No, I do not.'

'Are you close to them?'

'Yes and no.'

'What does that mean?' she asked.

He let out a frustrated sigh. 'Look, my parents do not have a particularly happy marriage. I do not spend much time with them for the simple reason I do not like hearing them bicker with each other all the time. It grates on me.'

'Why don't they get divorced?'

'They do not believe in divorce.'

'How ironic,' she said with an ironic twist to her mouth, 'That you—their only son—doesn't believe in marriage.'

'It is not that I have anything against marriage, Scarlett. I know of several very happy marriages where both parties love and respect each other.'

'But you don't want that for yourself.'

'No.'

Scarlett let her gaze fall away from the determined depths of his. 'I told you four years ago you'll end up a lonely old man.'

'I am prepared to risk a bit of late-life loneliness to have my freedom now.'

She brought her eyes back to his. 'So you go from one relationship to the other, a month with one woman, a week or two with another? That's such a shallow way to live.'

'You are entitled to your opinion, but it is not the way I see things.'

She threw him a disgusted look and said, 'Go on, tell me—what's the longest relationship you've ever had?'

His gaze meshed with hers for several heart-chugging seconds. The silence was so intense, Scarlett could hear the sound of her own breathing.

'It was the one I had with you, *cara*,' he said with a little smile. 'Three months, two days and nine-and-a-half hours.'

Scarlett's mouth went completely dry. 'You...you counted the days and hours?'

She wasn't completely sure, but she thought his crooked smile contained a hint of sadness. 'I missed you after you had gone,' he said. 'I was angry at first. Angry for days, weeks even, but then I kept finding things you had left behind—an earring or a little souvenir you had bought, and forgotten to put away with the rest of your things.'

She ran her tongue over her lips. 'What did you do with them?'

'I kept them.'

She frowned at him as he rose from the table. 'But...but why?'

He came around to help her to her feet, his fingers warm and vibrant on the bare skin of her arms. 'Do you know, that to this day I am still not sure,' he said, turning her to face him, his hands going to her waist, his fathomless gaze holding hers. 'Perhaps I always hoped we would see each other again.'

Scarlett felt her breath catch like a tiny fish-hook at the

back of her throat. 'Did-did you feel anything for me back then, Alessandro, anything at all other than desire?'

He lifted one hand from her waist and brushed the back of his bent knuckles over the curve of her cheek, his eyes now more brown than green. 'Why do you ask? You do not still have feelings for me, do you, *cara*?'

She didn't answer for the simple reason she couldn't get her voice to work. She had locked away her feelings for him four years ago, but her chest felt like it was going to explode with the effort of keeping them back.

His thumb stroked over the teeth marks on her lip in a tender caress. 'You are wavering, are you not?'

Her startled gaze flicked back to his. 'No…'

He smiled a sexy blood-heating-to-boiling-point smile. 'That did not sound very convincing, *tesore mio*.'

'*No,*' she said more stridently this time, although she shivered all over when he brought her hips up against his.

'Can you feel the effect you have on me?' he asked in a husky tone. 'How we still affect each other?'

Scarlett could, but she didn't want to admit it. She tried to put some space between their bodies, but his hold was both gentle and determined. She was breathing too hard and too shallowly to get her brain to work. Her body was taking over, just like it had all those years ago. One touch from him and she was going weak at the knees, her heart racing with excitement, her blood surging to all her pleasure points in preparation for the exquisite torture of his touch.

His head came down, and she did nothing to stop his lips making contact with hers. Instead she closed her eyes, a soft sigh escaping from her mouth into the warm, dark cavern of his as he held her captive under the searing pressure of his kiss.

His tongue searched for hers in a single commanding thrust that sent an earthquake-like reaction right through her. Aftershocks of pleasure reverberated throughout her body, each of her limbs beginning to tremble with the sheer force of being in his arms again.

His hands shaped her with the confidence of a lover who knew her body well and desired it greatly. She revelled in the possessive clamp of his teeth against her breast as he roughly freed it from the barrier of her clothes, the almost primitive action sending hot sparks of desire to every part of her body. His mouth suckled on her hotly, his tongue laving her nipple, his teeth grazing her again.

Somewhere at the blurry back of her conscience she knew she should be pushing him away, not clutching at him in passionate desperation, but there was nothing she could do to hold back her response. It was as if it was hard-wired into her system; every time he touched her he set her alight with burning need, just as he had done four years ago. One kiss had started something that was way beyond her capability to withstand.

When he lifted her skirt to her waist and searched for her hot, melting core she did nothing to resist him. Instead she gasped with mind-blowing pleasure as his fingers pushed aside the lace of her knickers to find their honeyed target, the movement so sensual, so devastatingly sexy, she arched upwards to have more of him.

'Please…*oh, please*…' she begged as he teased her mercilessly.

'You want me, *cara*?'

'Y-yes…' she panted as he brushed against the swollen pearl of her need.

He smiled a victor's smile as he cupped her face with his

hand. 'I knew you would not be able to resist,' he said. 'You are the same as you were four years ago—wanton and shameless in your quest for fulfilment.'

His words were enough to bring Scarlett back to earth with a jarring thud. She stepped out of his hold and smoothed down her skirt with what precious little dignity she had left. 'As far as I recall, this wasn't part of the contract,' she said with a cutting edge to her voice.

'I am prepared to pay double time for out-of-hours work,' he put in with suave smoothness.

She glared at him, affronted. 'You think you can afford *me*, Alessandro?'

His cynical smile cut through her like a scalpel. 'You can name your price, Scarlett. I will pay it to have you in my arms again. And, yes, I can afford you.' The dark gaze raked her mercilessly. 'Easily.'

She folded her arms across her body, more to stop one of them slapping that arrogant look off his face. She couldn't believe his audacity, to think he could buy her like the whore he thought she was. 'I want to go home,' she said with a petulant toss of her head. *'Now.'*

'You will go home when I say you can go home.'

She sent him a glowering look. 'You can't hold me here against my will.'

He stepped towards her, backing her against the wall as he stroked his hands down the length of her bare arms, his touch like silk sliding over a warm, smooth surface. 'But it will not be against your will, will it, *cara*?' he asked. 'I can see the longing in your eyes. You would be on that floor flat on your back by now, if your pride had not got in the way.'

Scarlett wanted to deny it, but knew he would never believe

her, not when she had allowed him to touch her so intimately just moments earlier.

She mentally cringed in shame. How could she have allowed herself to succumb to his lethal charm in such a degrading way? It confirmed all his misguided opinions of her as a shallow, money-hungry tart who would open her legs for the highest bidder.

'At least I have *some* measure of pride,' she tossed back after a tense pause.

His hazel gaze pinned hers. 'How much do you want to be my lover again?'

She flattened her spine against the wall. 'I told you, Alessandro, you can't afford me.'

His eyes hardened with chips of cold-green purpose. 'How much, Scarlett? How much to have you in my bed again for the time I am in Sydney?'

CHAPTER SEVEN

SCARLETT eyeballed him with gritty determination. 'It may have escaped your notice, but I don't have a "for sale" sign stamped on my forehead.'

His mouth tipped up at one corner. 'Like a lot of women I know, Scarlett, you have a price. But what you are doing by these delaying tactics is trying to drive up the price a little further, is it not?'

She sent him a caustic glare. 'I am *not* going to be used by you, not for any price.'

'It is a very clever manoeuvre,' he said as if she hadn't spoken. 'And well known in the circles I move in.'

'Yes, well, I don't care for the circles you move in,' she said primly. 'Your model friend is a case in point. She's looking for prestige and notoriety by hanging off your arm. I would have thought by now you would have been able to pick it up a mile off. She's after money and nothing else.'

'Velika has nothing to do with the arrangement we have made between ourselves,' he said.

Scarlett felt like stamping her foot. 'There *is* no arrangement between us!' she insisted.

He lifted one dark brow meaningfully. 'Aren't you forgetting something, Scarlett?'

She swallowed convulsively as she saw the flecks of brown in his eyes darken, her stomach turning over itself as he tilted her chin up with the point of one finger. 'You signed a contract, Scarlett, remember?' he said, his eyes locking on hers. 'Your business will fall over if you have to pay your way out of your contract with me.'

She ran the tip of her tongue over the dryness of her lips, her heart beginning to pick up its pace alarmingly. 'Are you…?' She cleared her throat when her voice dried up and began again. 'B-blackmailing me into your bed?'

His smile was slanted at a devastatingly sexy angle. 'Blackmail is rather a distasteful term, is it not? I was hoping you would agree to resume our affair without having to resort to using such underhand tactics,' he said. 'After all, you have made it very clear you are still attracted to me.'

'That's totally irrelevant!' she argued. 'Physical attraction to someone doesn't give automatic licence to have an affair with them. There's such a thing as self-control, you know.'

He ran his hands down her arms to encircle her wrists again, his long, strong fingers like twin bracelets of velvet-covered steel. 'I do not feel any self-control when I am around you, *cara*,' he said as his eyes held hers in the magnetic force-field of his gaze. 'I never did, and I sometimes wonder if I ever will.'

Scarlett could feel the slow melt of her bones under his touch, her belly doing tiny, jerky somersaults as each of his thumbs began stroking the sensitive undersides of her wrists. Desire pulsed hot and thickly through her bloodstream, her skin tingling in response to his drugging caresses. Her legs were weakening beneath her, and she felt the involuntary loosening of her spine as one of his hands went to the lower curve of her back and brought her up against his hardness.

'Kiss me, Scarlett,' he commanded softly. 'Kiss me the way you used to do, with your whole body and soul.'

Scarlett's gaze dropped to his mouth and her belly did another sudden flip-turn. 'I-I don't think—'

His hand at her back pressed her even closer. 'What are you frightened of, *tesore mio*?' he asked.

She moistened her lips with a tentative movement of her tongue, in case it accidentally brushed his mouth hovering so close to hers. 'I-I'm not frightened,' she said, even though fear had already thickened her throat so she could barely swallow.

His lips nibbled at the side of her mouth, so close to the tingling fullness of her bottom lip she felt her legs begin to tremble, his warm breath dancing over her face and mouth tantalisingly. She felt the brush of his tongue against her cheek, and then along the seam of her mouth, the sensual movement making all hope of resisting him impossible.

She gave a little whimper and opened her mouth under the next sweep of his tongue, taking him inside to her moist warmth, mating with him in a dancing duel that mimicked what their bodies had done so well together in the past. Passion flared like a bush fire, the hot, licking flames sending Scarlett's heart-rate soaring as his pelvis ground against hers, his hardness against her velvet softness making every scrap of sense she possessed move even further out of reach of reason and rationality. She clung to him, her mouth on fire beneath the passionate onslaught of his, her teeth nipping at him as he nipped at her, her tongue flicking as his thrust, her body turning to liquid as his grew rock-hard and insistent.

His hands went back to her breasts, pushing aside her scooped neckline to gain access, his mouth a hot brand as he sucked on each engorged nipple in turn. Scarlett was vaguely aware of crying out in pleasure, partially aware too of digging her fingers into the thick hair of his scalp as she arched her spine to have more of his heat against her.

'You are just as passionate as you were before,' Alessandro said against her neck, his tone husky with desire. 'Perhaps even more so.'

Scarlett pulled away from him with an effort, her conscience an unbearable burden. She couldn't do this. Not while he thought she was only coming to him in exchange for money. It sullied everything they had shared in the past. It tainted everything she had given of herself. She had adored him; she had worshipped him in every way imaginable. To be reduced to a mere plaything was anathema to her.

'What is wrong, *cara*?' Alessandro asked.

She moistened her dry lips. 'Please take me home,' she said, tears shining in her eyes. *'Please...'*

Alessandro frowned as he considered talking her into staying a little longer. He knew it would not take much to persuade her—she was clearly as aroused as he was—but something about those tears in her grey-blue eyes warned him he had pushed her a little too far too soon. He had plenty of time; after all, the Arlington project would take several months to complete. He would no doubt have numerous opportunities to convince her to be his mistress again. He would have to be patient, that was all. He had waited this long; he could wait a little longer.

He reached for his keys and gave her a twisted smile. 'Come, *tesore mio*,' he said. 'I have found out what I needed to know in any case.'

Scarlett wanted to ask him what he meant, but she had a feeling she already knew. She followed him out to his car and sat in a miserable, guilt-stricken silence as he drove her back to her tiny flat.

He walked her to the door and waited until she had unlocked it, before he bent down to press a barely-there kiss to both of her cheeks. 'Sweet dreams,' he said. 'I will see you soon, no?'

Scarlett's throat was almost too tight to reply. 'Y-yes…'

Once Roxanne had left a few minutes later Scarlett went into her son's bedroom. One of his little arms was flung over the edge of the bed, the other clutching a matchbox car close to his face. She gently unpeeled his little fingers, her heart contracting painfully when she found a shiny-black Maserati lying there…

'Phone for you,' Roxanne said when Scarlett came inside the studio the next morning. 'It's Alessandro. By the way, I told him you're not involved with Dylan. And you can stop looking at me like that. He asked and I answered.'

Scarlett was still scowling as she picked up her extension. 'Hello, Scarlett Fitzpatrick speaking.'

'So you have decided to concentrate your efforts on the biggest return, eh, *cara*?'

'That is a despicable thing to say,' she said, turning her back on Roxanne.

'Are you missing me, *cara*?'

Scarlett felt her heart miss a beat at that low, velvet drawl, her stomach crawling all over again with desire.

He suddenly laughed, the deep rumble sending tiny shivers of reaction to the core of her being. 'You cannot help yourself, eh, Scarlett? You want me even though you do not want to do so. It is the same for me. I did not think I would feel this way about you, but I do.'

Scarlett held her breath. 'What are you saying?'

'I am saying I want to see you tomorrow night when I get back from Melbourne.'

She flattened her lips together, stalling as she tried to withstand the temptation.

'I will come to your house, if you like,' he offered. 'My flight back to Sydney is not a late one.'

Her hand tightened on the receiver. She wanted more time to prepare Matthew for a visit from his father. She wanted Alessandro to know for certain he *was* Matthew's father when they met for the first time. She had been lucky before, as Matthew had been fast asleep in bed and Alessandro hadn't seemed to notice the photos on the wall unit, but if he came around for any length of time…

'Umm…I don't think that's such a great idea,' she said, knowing it sounded pathetically lame. 'I'd rather meet on neutral ground.'

'I will book a hotel room and then no one will disturb us.'

'No! That's sound so…so terribly tacky,' she said and releasing a breath of resignation, added, 'I'll come to your house…after I've put my son to bed. But I insist on making my own way there.'

'All right,' he said. 'If you insist.'

'What about Velika Vanovic?' she asked after a tiny but tense pause.

'What about her?' His tone was impersonal and cool.

'She's your current mistress, isn't she?'

'She is not relevant to us, Scarlett.'

'Are you still seeing her and sleeping with her?'

'Why are you so interested?' he asked.

'I don't like sharing.'

He laughed again. 'You are so delightfully transparent. I like that about you. I like it a lot.'

'And yet you think I lied to you about our son.'

The silence this time was taut as a wire strained to its limits.

'I will see you tomorrow evening, Scarlett,' he said in a curt tone.

'I might not be here,' she said with reckless abandon. 'I might change my mind at the last minute.'

'You will be there,' he said, and ended the call before she could contradict him.

Roxanne came over to Scarlett's desk. 'Let me guess, you want me to babysit again, right?'

Scarlett bit her lip and nodded.

Roxanne gave her shoulder a tiny squeeze. 'You're doing the right thing, honey,' she said. 'You have to sort this out one way or the other, and now's the time to do it.'

The following evening Scarlett stood on the doorstep of Alessandro's house with legs that trembled as she heard his footsteps approach the front door to answer her summons.

She clutched her folder to her chest and forced her eyes to meet his as he opened the door. 'I have some preliminary mock-ups for you to look over,' she said, nervously moistening her mouth.

'Come and show me what you have been up to,' he said with an unfathomable smile.

Scarlett followed him to where he had drinks and nibbles set out and, pushing her reservations to one side, took a glass of white wine and sat next to him on one of the sumptuous leather sofas. She took a tiny sip, trying not to notice how close his thigh was to hers. She could see the bunching of his muscles as he leaned forward for the bowl of crisps, her stomach beginning to prickle with desire at the thought of those long, strong legs entrapping hers, the way they had done in the past.

'Do you want some?'

Scarlett blinked at him vacuously.

He smiled as he held the bowl under her nose. 'You have gone all glassy-eyed on me, *cara*,' he said. 'What is going on in that beautiful blonde head of yours, mmm?'

Scarlett wondered he couldn't see what was going on for himself. She felt as if her need for him was written all over her skin, every fine pore ached to feel the glide of his hands on her flesh. Her cheeks felt hot, indeed her whole body felt as if it was smouldering, and she knew one touch from him would send her into flames.

She put her glass on the coffee table and began to get to her feet. 'Maybe I shouldn't have come here tonight…'

One of his hands came down over hers and held her fast. 'No, Scarlett,' he insisted. 'Do not leave.'

Scarlett looked at their joined hands and felt a feathery sensation run up her spine. Her breasts began to tighten beneath the soft lace of her bra as his thumb began to stroke her wrist, her pulse going like a threshing machine as he pulled her closer to bring his mouth into contact with hers.

She tasted wine and salt and sex, a devastating combination that left her with no hope of resisting. It was as if her body was specifically programmed to respond to him and him alone. She kissed him back without reserve, her tongue tangling with his in a sensual dance of dangerous desires finally unleashed. She felt the increasing urgency in him as he pushed her back to the cushioned comfort of the sofa, his weight coming over her, his erection nudging at her intimately as his hands went to her breasts.

She drew in a sharp little breath as he shaped her through

the thin fabric of her dress—but her breathing stalled altogether when he deftly unzipped her and unclipped her bra, so he could have his mouth on her bare skin. His lips closed over one tight nipple, making her back arch, and her toes curl so much her shoes fell to the carpeted floor with two soft little thuds.

He took her other nipple and suckled hard, the drawing of his mouth on her flesh making her whole body writhe in response.

'I want you, Scarlett,' he said as he removed the rest of her clothes before starting on his own. 'I want you so badly I cannot think of anything else.'

She looked down and touched him, almost reverently. He was so hard, so fully aroused. She wanted to reach down and taste him, to feel him move within the moistness of her mouth, to feel his control straining at the leash as she subjected him to one of the most intimate acts of all between lovers.

'If you want me to stop then you had better tell me now,' he said, even as he separated her tender folds in preparation for his entry.

She answered by kissing him on the mouth, her tongue meeting his in a dance of mutual desire that left words totally unnecessary. She felt him surge fully into her warmth, the thickness of him after so long making her wince slightly as her slim body accommodated him.

He pulled back and looked down at her in concern. 'Am I hurting you?'

'No…'

'Am I going too fast for you?'

She shook her head, unable to speak for the emotion clogging her throat. It felt so good to have him so deep and warm and hard inside her. Her body had missed him so much;

for nearly four years she had lain awake at night, aching for exactly this, feeling his flesh on her flesh, his skin on hers.

He brushed her mouth with his in a kiss that was as light as air but as hot as fire. 'I have been going mad with the need to do this,' he groaned, easing himself inside her gently. 'You feel so perfect.'

Scarlett let out a breathless gasp of pleasure as he filled her completely, his slow, gently rocking motion making her want him harder and faster. She clutched at his buttocks with her fingers, and he responded by upping his pace until she was writhing against him uninhibitedly, her legs like jelly as she felt each hard thrust bring her closer and closer to the release she craved with all her being.

Suddenly she was there, her body exploding with an orgasm so intense she felt as if she had momentarily lost consciousness. Wave after wave of pleasure swamped her being, her nerves twitching and jumping with the aftershocks of such a cataclysmic response to his love-making.

She felt him prepare for his final plunge into oblivion, the tension in his muscles building and building, before he thrust forward with a groan of pure ecstasy.

The silence pulsed for a moment or two as Scarlett tried to get her breathing back under control.

'Scarlett…' Alessandro said, lifting her chin with the pad of his index finger, his hazel eyes taking in the creeping colour staining her cheeks. 'Do not be ashamed of what just happened between us.'

Her teeth began to savage her lip. 'It shouldn't have happened. I can't believe I let things go that far…'

His hands came down on the tops of her shoulders. 'Listen to me, *cara*,' he said. 'I wanted that to happen. We both did.

We are both consenting adults who have a fierce attraction for each other. Why not enjoy it while it lasts?'

She slipped from beneath his hold and, scooping up her dress, fumbled her way back into it. 'I-I can't do this, Alessandro…' she said, her voice catching over the words. 'It's not what I want for my life.'

'What do you want for your life?' he asked after a beat or two of heavy silence.

She turned to look at him again, her expression so sad it pained him to see it. 'I want to get married to a man who loves and adores me,' she said. 'I want a normal life. I don't want a short-term affair with someone I no longer…' she hesitated for a fraction of a second '…love.'

'You might not love me, but you certainly desire me,' he said. 'Or are you going to deny that after what we just shared?'

'No…of course I'm not going to deny it,' she said, shifting her eyes from the determined probe of his. 'I am still attracted to you…' She bit her lip again before adding, 'Much more than I realized.'

He stepped towards her again and captured her waist with his hands. 'I want you back in my life, Scarlett,' he said with an implacable edge to his voice. 'I want you like I've wanted no other woman.'

She lifted her gaze to meet his. 'But for how long? You're well known for your fly-by-night relationships, Alessandro. I can't do that, living holding my breath as if each day could be the last we have together.'

'I cannot answer precisely,' he said, dropping his hands from her waist. 'It depends on how things go with the Arlington redevelopment…and other things.'

'I suppose by other things you mean your current mistress,

Velika Vanovic?' Scarlett asked with a scathing set to her mouth.

He gave her a level look. 'I am no longer involved with Velika Vanovic. You are the person I am now involved with, and after what just happened here I am not going to give you up without a fight.'

'But you said you weren't going to blackmail me any more,' she said as the pit of her stomach began to quake in alarm in case he changed his mind. 'Surely it is up to me whether this goes any further?'

His expression communicated nothing but iron-clad determination as he reached for her again. 'I do not need to blackmail you. I can see how much you want me. You have already proven it.'

'No,' she said, making a vain effort to push him away—but somehow her hands wouldn't cooperate, instead clutching at him with clawing need. 'I don't want to be involved with you again.'

'Yes you do, Scarlett,' he said, beginning to nibble on her earlobe in the way that made her spine instantly turn to liquid. 'You want me again. Once is never enough for you, or for me. I am already hard again.' He captured one of her hands and placed it on the hard ridge between his legs. 'Do not leave me in this state, *tesore mio*,' he groaned. 'I want you right now.'

Scarlett's fingers began stroking him almost of their own volition, the temptation of his body too much to withstand. How could she possibly deny herself the magic of his lovemaking? It was all she had ever wanted from the moment she had met him—to be in his arms, spinning out of control with the passion that constantly smouldered between them.

He groaned again. His teeth gritted as he fought for control, his head thrown back as she sank to her knees in front of him, her soft breath wafting over him tantalizingly, before she began stroking him with the tip of her tongue. His hands went to her head, his fingers delving into her hair as she slowly tortured him, each moist glide of her tongue taking him that much closer to the point of no return. She felt the power she had over him and it excited her, just as much if not more than it had done in the past.

His fingers dug deeper into her scalp. 'No, *cara*, I cannot take any more,' he said, breathing heavily.

Scarlett kept on caressing him, stroking then sucking in turn, until he exploded with a muttered curse, his body sagging against her once it was over.

She straightened, and was about to step backwards when he stalled her by encircling one of her wrists with his hand. 'No,' he said. 'This is a two-way street, Scarlett, remember? Just like in the past, you do not get to do that to me unless I am allowed to return the favour.'

Scarlett pulled ineffectually at his hold but her heart wasn't in it, and she could tell he knew it. She drew in a gasping little breath as he picked her up in his arms and carried her to the bedroom she had designed only months ago, her excitement building as his eyes burned into hers with sensual promise.

'You are so very sensual, Scarlett,' he said as he joined her on the bed, his weight pressing her into the mattress. 'I cannot get enough of you. I have craved this for so long—to see you again, to feel you again, to make love to you again as we used to do. I have missed what we had so much.'

'I've missed it too,' she said in a soft whisper as she stroked the lean line of his jaw. 'You have no idea how much.'

He traced the point of his index finger from her belly button to the tiny landing-strip of dark-blonde hair that shielded her femininity. 'I have never forgotten the taste of you,' he said in a low growl. 'God, the nights I have lain awake thinking of the taste of you.'

Scarlett drew in a ragged breath as he bent his head to her moist warmth, his tongue moving against her swollen point of pleasure with exquisite expertise. She had no control over her response; it shook her from the inside out, each movement of his tongue sending her into a vortex of feeling that reverberated throughout every part of her body.

He moved back over her, his thighs entangled with hers in an erotic embrace as he entered her silken warmth in a strong, gliding thrust that sent sparks of pleasure from her head to her curling toes.

His mouth came down on hers, the sexy saltiness of her body mingled with his warm breath as he played with her lips, tugging at them with his teeth, teasing her tongue into a passionate duel. She nibbled at his bottom lip, sucking on it, pulling at it with her teeth and then sweeping over it with the tip of her tongue, the deep groans of pleasure he was emitting from the back of his throat thrilling her, and inciting her to do it all over again and again.

He responded by increasing his pace, his body driving into hers with tender force, the thick, hard length of him caressing her in all the right places. She only had to tilt her hips upwards to feel the first flicker of release, the second and third quickly following, until she lost count as she shuddered her way through another mind-blowing orgasm.

Her body was still pulsing with the aftershocks when she felt his whole body tensing above hers in that final second or two before he finally lost control. His face contorted with pleasure as he sucked in a harsh breath before releasing it in a rush as he spilled himself with explosive power.

In the silence that followed Scarlett felt her conscience

begin to prod at her. She wasn't a sleep-around sort of woman, she never had been. She had only had one lover apart from Alessandro and now, with the responsibilities of a small child, she could never treat any relationship with a man as just physical. And certainly not this man—the father of her son.

Alessandro propped himself up on his elbows to look down at her. 'This feels so right,' he said with a wistful look coming and going in his dark, intense gaze. 'This part always felt so right between us.'

She compressed her lips, trying not to show how emotionally affected she was. 'But I want much more than you are prepared to give…'

He got off the bed, reached for a bathrobe, and tied it around his waist. 'I have told you the rules,' he said with a curt edge to his voice. 'This is all I can offer you, Scarlett. Believe me—you should be content with that.'

Scarlett reached for her wrinkled clothes and struggled back into them, hoping she wouldn't betray herself by crying uncontrollably. 'I need to go home. It's getting late.'

He came from behind and held her against his solid, hard male warmth. Her breath whooshed out of her lungs as she felt his growing arousal behind her, the thin barrier of her clothes not enough to stop her from responding with a soft whimper of pleasure as his mouth began to nuzzle against her neck, and his hands cupped her already tingling, peaking breasts.

'You do not really want to go home right at this very minute, do you, Scarlett?'

'No…' she whispered huskily as he turned her to face him, his mouth coming down to hers. 'God help me but, no, I don't…'

CHAPTER EIGHT

ROXANNE WAS out on a call at a client's house when Alessandro arrived at the studio the next morning. Scarlett heard his car first, and a ticklish feeling ran up her spine as she swivelled on her office chair to look out the window.

She watched as he unfolded himself from the vehicle. His hair looked like black satin in the morning sunshine, his lean face cleanly shaven, his dark pin-striped trousers emphasising the length of his legs and trimness of his waist, and his light-blue business shirt highlighting the olive tone of his skin.

Her stomach flipped and then flopped as he stepped onto the pavement, his eyes meeting hers through the window. She pushed herself away from the desk and stood up as he came in the door, her hands going to her thighs to smooth down her skirt.

He moved across the small space of the studio and, cupping her cheeks with both hands, kissed her thoroughly. Scarlett breathed in the heady fragrance of musky male, sharp citrus and tortuous temptation. All her carefully rehearsed reasons for not agreeing to a resumption of their relationship were suddenly deleted from her brain as his tongue flicked erotically against hers.

Still cupping her face in his hands, he lifted his mouth off hers and smiled down at her. 'I knew you would be here waiting for me,' he said.

She screwed up her mouth at him. 'It *is* my studio after all,' she pointed out. 'Where else would I be?'

He tucked a strand of silver-blonde hair behind her ear, the brush of his fingers against her face making her tremble deep inside. 'You are still fighting it, yes?'

She lowered her gaze. 'I don't want to get hurt…'

He brought her chin up. 'I am only involved with you, Scarlett. You have my word.'

Scarlett wondered if she was being fobbed off. How could she tell? He was a notorious playboy; women flocked to him wherever he went. He had said it himself: he wasn't the settling-down type.

'If you do not believe me, read this morning's paper,' he added.

Scarlett's gaze went to the folded newspaper lying on Roxanne's desk. They usually had a quick flick through it during their coffee and lunch breaks, but with Roxanne still out at a client's house, and with the number of calls Scarlett had had to make in her partner's absence, there hadn't been time to even put on the kettle.

'There is a short article about us on page three,' he informed her.

'About us?' she asked, her eyes going wide. 'What do you mean "about us"?'

He walked over to Roxanne's desk, picked up the paper and opened it to the page where a small paragraph was headed: *Billionaire Hotelier involved with Local Interior Designer.*

Scarlett read the accompanying paragraph with her heart kicking like a wild brumby in her chest. It was only a few words about her and the studio, and thankfully no photograph accompanied it. It simply stated she was the new love interest of Alessandro Marciano.

She closed the paper and handed it back to him. 'Well, that just goes to show you can't believe everything you read in the press,' she said with an embittered look. 'I am not your love interest, am I, Alessandro? I am just someone to sleep with, someone to slake your lust with. You just want a fill-in affair while you are here—let's not go calling it anything else.'

His hazel eyes caught and held hers. 'Love is a favourite word of yours, is it not?'

'It's not just a word,' she said. 'It's a feeling, and in some ways almost a way of life. You've always shunned it, but you don't know what living is all about until you allow yourself to love someone more than life itself.'

She swallowed as he stepped towards her again, his hand tilting her face so she couldn't avoid his penetrating gaze.

'Love is a very cruel mistress,' he said with a rueful twist to his mouth. 'She takes hold of you, and then dumps you when you least expect it.' He released her chin to brush the curve of her cheek with the pad of his thumb, the touch so light she wondered if she had imagined it. 'I learned not to love a number of years ago, long before I met you,' he continued. 'I decided it was not worth the suffering once that person is no longer with you.'

'That seems a very selfish way of viewing things. What if the person you loved didn't leave?'

He dropped his hand from her face and moved back from her. 'Sometimes there is no way to control such things, Scarlett.'

'Alessandro...' She took a step towards him, but his eyes had already shifted from hers and before she could stop him he moved past her to look at the screen-saver that had come up on her computer. She watched with baited breath as he looked at the montage of images of Matthew she had constructed, his body becoming as still as a lifeless statue as his eyes roved each and every photo.

Every milestone was there—the first ultrasound picture, the first few minutes after birth, Matthew's first tooth, his first birthday, his first wobbly steps, even his recent third birthday with the racing-car cake she had made for him.

The silence stretched to the point of pain.

Alessandro was not aware of his hands gripping the edge of the desk until he finally registered his fingers were numb. His heart was beating, but too fast and too hard. His stomach contents were liquefying, his vision was blurring. He couldn't swallow, he couldn't breathe, he couldn't even think.

'His name is Matthew.' Scarlett's soft voice carved through his swirling thoughts. 'He turned three a couple of months ago.'

Alessandro counted back the months and gripped the desk even tighter. It couldn't be true. It was a lie. He had seen the test results. He was infertile, as planned.

But the child *looked* like him.

God, he even looks like Marco, Alessandro thought with a gut-wrenching pang of grief that he'd deluded himself into thinking he had locked down long ago.

Somehow he found the wherewithal to turn away from the computer screen and face Scarlett. His heart was still doing leap-frogs in his chest but, seeing her there, standing so still and silently before him, was like a stake being driven right through his body.

'He's yours, Alessandro, even if you don't want to ever acknowledge it,' she said, holding his gaze determinedly.

He scraped a hand through his hair and drew in a breath that scalded his throat. 'I need proof. I am sorry if it offends you, but I need to have proof. It is…' He swallowed deeply. 'It is important.'

She gave him one of her scathing looks as she folded her arms across her body. 'I believe you can buy a DNA kit off the internet. I am quite willing to allow you to use it.'

She wasn't supposed to say that, Alessandro thought with another wave of dread. Not if she had lied to him. The way she had suggested a test the other day and then instantly backed down had made him think she was still lying. But there was no way she would give him the go-ahead for a test that would prove without a doubt who was the child's father. Besides, she'd had three years to try and force a paternity test on him and yet she hadn't done so. The legal system was full of such cases these days—men who had been paying out large sums of money for children had begun to fight back, insisting on proof the children they were supporting were actually biologically theirs.

'I don't know what to say…' He hated admitting it, but it was true. He was lost for words. He had never been in a situation like this before. He had always prided himself on being in control, which was why he had insisted on having a vasectomy in the first place. He didn't want a repeat of what had happened to Marco. He couldn't bear to put a child of his through it, not knowing what he knew about himself and his family.

'"Sorry for not believing you" would be a very good start,' she said with crispness in her tone.

He swallowed again to clear his throat. 'I will have to save that for when I know for sure.'

She rolled her eyes in disdain. 'You can't do it, can you?

You can't even for a moment harbour the possibility that you got it wrong.'

His jaw felt so tight he thought his teeth were going to crack. 'Do you have any idea of what this is like for me? *Do you?*' he asked.

She glared at him with chips of grey-blue fire in her gaze. 'You're not going to get the sympathy vote from me, Alessandro. I was the one who carried your child for nine miserable months, and delivered him after an eighteen-hour labour without his father there to support me.

'Don't talk to me about how this is for you. You don't even know half of what it's been like for me. I have struggled to provide for my child. I've had to put him in crèche when I would much rather be at home with him, but what other choice did I have? I can't even afford to send him to the school of my choice when the time comes, because his arrogant, always-right untrusting bastard of a father wouldn't accept that he might have somehow got it wrong.'

Alessandro felt as if an avalanche had hit him. The first glimmer of tears in her eyes was like the blunt end of a telegraph pole hitting him in the mid-section. He moved towards her, but she swung away and snapped up a tissue from a pretty little box with primroses on it. *Funny, the little inconsequential things you noticed when everything else was spinning out of control,* he thought as he watched her wipe at her eyes and discreetly blow her nose.

'I'll arrange to see a doctor tomorrow,' he said. 'It might take a day or two to get the sperm-test results back from Pathology.'

Scarlett turned and looked at him with a puzzled frown. 'Sperm tests?'

His eyes were full of pain as they met hers. 'I had a vasectomy performed when I was twenty-eight years old. I was declared infertile three months later.'

Scarlett stared at him in a stunned silence. No wonder he had denied fathering a child so vehemently. What man wouldn't have reacted in exactly the same way? He had believed himself to be incapable of fathering a child; he had taken the necessary steps to ensure it would never happen. Looking at it from his angle, he had every right to be suspicious—although a part of her still felt he should have trusted her regardless.

'Scarlett…' he said, dragging a hand through his hair, his expression still tortured with anguish. 'I never thought something like this could happen. It never once occurred to me that it could. The chances of it must be a million to one at least.'

Her slim shoulders began to shake, and he moved across the room. His hands came down on her shoulders and turned her to face him. Emotion clogged his throat at the grey-blue of her tear-washed eyes. He realised then that, if he had ever had a choice in the matter, she would have been the mother of his children. She would make the perfect mother. She was gentle and nurturing, and yet strong and determined—so like his own mother used to be until life dealt her such a cruel hand. His mother was not the same mother he had adored, even though Marco had been buried long ago.

He hardly realised he was doing it as he lifted Scarlett's chin with the point of his finger. 'If you do not want to continue with the project I will cancel the contract. You will not incur any expense as a result.'

She bit her lip so hard he was sure bright-red blood was going to spring from it. He brushed his thumb against her teeth and her lips trembled in response.

'It's all right,' she said on an expelled breath. 'I will do it.

But I want you to know I'm not doing it for you or for me, but for Roxanne.'

He lifted one brow quizzically.

'She's worked so hard for what we've built up,' Scarlett explained. 'We both have, but I've been a bit hamstrung with my commitments to Matthew. She's been so good, and I don't want to let her down.'

Alessandro placed his hands on the top of her shoulders and gently squeezed. 'We will sort it out, Scarlett, do not worry.'

She lowered her gaze. 'He's so like you…' she whispered.

He closed his eyes against the sudden and unexpected sting of tears; his chest felt like a clamp had been placed on his heart and lungs.

'I wanted to send you photos,' she went on, her voice still barely audible. 'So many times I wanted to prove to you how like you he is. He even does that little thing you do when you sleep.'

'What thing?' His voice sounded like a croak, but at least he had been able to get it to work.

'He sprawls all over the bed,' she said. 'With his arms and legs everywhere. It's so cute.'

Alessandro stood in silence as he breathed in the scent of her silver-blonde hair; it had always reminded him of the fragrance of sun-warmed jasmine.

Something inside his chest began to loosen, like a too-tight knot that had resisted all attempts to be untied for years.

What if the thing he suspected had indeed happened? Would she agree to resume their relationship on a more permanent basis for the child's sake, or would she always resent him for not believing her in the first place?

He had shut off his feelings for her four years ago, but he

knew it wouldn't take much to switch them back on again. Hadn't last night proved how close to the wind he was sailing? He could feel the tug of desire even now as she stood silently in his embrace. His body was stirring against her; she surely could feel it, although so far she hadn't made a move to step backwards from him.

His mind started to run with the possibilities—but then he was brought back to earth with a jarring thud as he remembered there was the other issue of the child's health. He was only three now, but Marco had shown signs not much earlier than that…

She eased herself out of his hold and, without looking at him, tucked a strand of hair behind her left ear. 'I'm sorry…this must be so hard for you,' she said. 'I mean, learning about the existence of a child you never wanted.'

It was on the tip of his tongue to say how much he would have loved children of his own, perfectly healthy, robust children—a boy, a girl, what did it matter? He had never understood parents who claimed to have a preference for one or the other sex. As long as it was healthy was all that mattered, but that was one thing he could not guarantee.

It had been taken out of his hands on the day he'd been born.

'Yes,' he said, feeling his chest go down in a sigh. 'It is hard, but we will know for sure in a day or so.'

It was totally the wrong thing to say; he knew it as soon as he said it. She stiffened like someone who had been sprayed with quick-setting glue, her mouth went tight, her eyes turned to blue chips of ice, and her bitterness cut through the air like a sharpened blade.

'How typical,' she said, 'how absolutely typical.'

'What I meant to say was—'

She stalked across to the door and held it open, the tiny bell tinkling in startled protest. 'What you meant to say was you still don't believe me,' she bit out. 'There's still a small part of you that won't accept Matthew as your son. Now please leave, before I change my mind about the DNA test or the contract.'

It was not in Alessandro's nature to back down. He had fought long and hard for many things in his life, and certainly being dismissed by a tiny silver-blonde virago was not something he was used to accepting. But the set to her mouth told him it was probably a good time to leave.

He brought two of his fingers up to his mouth and pressed his lips against them in a mimic of a kiss, before placing them on the stiff but somehow still-soft bow of her mouth. 'I will be back in a couple of days with the results,' he said.

'I can tell you the results right now,' she replied, swiping at her mouth as if he had tainted her with his touch.

He held her embittered gaze with determination. 'I have to be sure, Scarlett. I know it's hard for you, but you have to understand my position on this. You have no doubt at all he is your child. You physically gave birth to him, you needed no other evidence—but I am afraid that I do.'

She spun away with a frustrated sound that was somewhere between a scornful snort and a sigh. 'Please leave,' she said. 'There's no point in continuing this conversation until you have what you want.'

But I can never have what I want, Alessandro thought as he drove away a short time later, his eyes fixed on the road ahead in case he was tempted to look back.

I can never have what I want.

CHAPTER NINE

'ARE YOU sure?' Alessandro asked Dr Underwood two days later. 'There is absolutely *no* doubt?'

Dr Underwood shook his head. 'No doubt at all, Mr Marciano. Your sperm count is positive. I don't know who did your vasectomy, but from the test results we've received it clearly wasn't entirely successful. That doesn't mean the surgeon was incompetent, by any means, it's just that—as I am sure he or she would have explained at the time—there is about a one percent failure-rate for the procedure. That's why we insist on the three negative sperm-counts after three months post-surgery.'

Alessandro frowned. 'But I had three counts done in Italy and they were all negative. What are the chances of a rejoin after three negative readings?'

Dr Underwood scratched at his closely cropped greying beard for a moment. 'It's less likely,' he said. 'At least half the failures occur in the first three months after the operation, but the rest can occur up to five years later.'

Alessandro stared at him, his heart chugging, his skin breaking out in a sweat in spite of the air-conditioned comfort of the consulting room.

He was a father.

Something he had never intended to happen had happened.

He was the father of a three-year-old boy.

Oh, dear God, what had he done?

Dr Underwood leaned forward on his desk. 'You can always have the procedure redone. I can organise a referral to a surgeon for you.'

'Yes,' Alessandro said without hesitation. 'Yes, I would like you to do that. I want it done as soon as possible.'

The doctor's brows moved closer together. 'You were quite young when you had it originally performed. You are what age now…?' He looked down at his notes. 'Only just thirty-three. You seem very determined about this. Do you want to discuss it with a professional, such as a counsellor or psychologist, first?'

'No, I made up my mind a long time ago that I do not want to have children.'

The doctor scribbled on his notepad and, tearing the page off, placed it in an envelope and handed it to Alessandro. 'Let's hope this time it works,' he said with a crooked smile.

'Yes,' Alessandro said, rising to his feet. 'Thank you for your time.'

Dr Underwood pushed back his chair and got to his feet as well. 'If you change your mind at any time about seeing a counsellor, just let me know. You know…' He gave a somewhat philosophical smile this time. 'Sometimes these things are just meant to happen.'

Alessandro didn't respond. He couldn't. His voice was trapped somewhere deep in the middle of his chest, where he could feel a sensation like a hand squeezing his heart with cruelly tight fingers.

* * *

'You've been staring at that phone for the last two hours,' Roxanne said. 'He will ring or contact you when he feels ready to do so.'

Scarlett chomped on her bottom lip for the hundredth time that afternoon. 'I'm so confused,' she confessed. 'I've been so angry towards him for all this time, but then when I stop and think about what he's going through I feel terrible. If only he had *told* me at the time. I would have insisted on a test. I feel partially to blame now for all he's missed out on. I shouldn't have let it go. I shouldn't have let my experiences with my father interfere with Alessandro's rights as a father.'

Roxanne came over and perched on her desk, as was her custom. 'Why did he have the cut done in the first place?' she asked. 'Does he generally hate kids, or is there some other reason?'

Scarlett leaned back in her chair and blew out a breath. 'I don't know,' she said. 'I feel a bit ashamed to admit it, but we never really got around to talking about those sorts of issues. Besides, I always knew I was more in love with him than he was with me. He never said the three magic words. I think he was more interested in a short-term affair. He never once mentioned the future—it was as if he didn't expect to have one, certainly not with me.'

'He's absolutely gorgeous looking,' Roxanne said, and, glancing at the screen saver on Scarlett's computer, added, 'Matthew's the spitting image of him.'

Scarlett put her head in her hands and let out another sigh. 'What am I going to tell Matthew?' she asked. 'He thinks his father is dead.'

'I think the truth always works best with kids,' Roxanne said. 'I hated finding out I was adopted at the age of ten. I should have been told when I was much younger. I know

Matthew's only three, but he's one smart kid. He understands far more than you give him credit for.'

Scarlett dragged her head up to meet her friend's gaze. 'You're right,' she said. 'I need to tell him, at least to prepare him in some way, for once Alessandro finds out the truth I'm sure he will want to take control.'

'What sort of control are you talking about?' Roxanne asked with a little frown of concern.

Scarlett's bottom lip suffered another indentation with her teeth. 'I'm not sure…but knowing him as I do I think he will want to have things his way. He's been so confident for so long that Matthew's not his child. It will be a blow to his ego to find out he is wrong.'

'Do you think this is just about ego?' Roxanne asked with another frown. 'Most men are proud of the fact they can cut the mustard, or whatever the saying is.'

Scarlett couldn't help smiling, but it faded as she answered, 'I don't really know. I've met plenty of men who were adamant they didn't want children. I've met women just as strident about avoiding motherhood. As I said earlier, Alessandro and I never really got around to discussing the marriage-and-babies thing. I wanted to, many times, but you know how it is with a new relationship—you tread so carefully in case you scare them off.'

'But weren't you on the Pill?' Roxanne asked.

Scarlett shifted her gaze from the probe of her friend's. 'Yes and no.'

'What does that mean?'

'It basically means no.'

Roxanne rolled her eyes. 'Yeah, that's what I figured.'

'I was young and naïve,' Scarlett said in her own defence.

'I didn't for a moment expect to become involved in a full-on relationship while I was overseas.'

'Yes, well, someone should have warned you about men like Alessandro,' Roxanne said with a wry look.

Scarlett turned to look at the screen saver and sighed again. 'He's missed out on so much… Maybe I should have sent him some photos right from the start. I wanted to many times, but then I thought of the way he threw me out on the street that night and I changed my mind.'

Roxanne placed a hand on her shoulder. 'It's not your fault, Scarlett. You did your best and he refused to listen. Maybe it had to happen this way.'

Scarlett gave another deep sigh. 'How am I going to tell Matthew his father is alive?'

Roxanne gave her shoulder a little squeeze. 'You'll think of a way.'

'How was crèche today, darling?' Scarlett asked as she lifted Matthew into his evening bath.

Matthew's bottom lip came forward slightly as he settled amongst the bubbles. 'Robert taked my car off me, one of my favourite ones.'

'Robert *took* your car off you,' she corrected automatically. 'That's terrible, darling. Did Mrs Bennett or Miss Fielding get it back for you?'

He shook his head and his little shoulders went down. 'No.'

'I'll have a word to them about it tomorrow,' she promised. 'Maybe Robert doesn't have many toys and really enjoyed playing with yours.'

'I don't want to go there any more,' he said, big tears

forming in his hazel eyes as he looked up at her. 'I want to come to work wif you.'

'Darling, you know that's impossible. We've talked about this before, lots of times.'

Another little sigh puffed out of his mouth. 'I know…'

She took a break to prepare herself. 'Matthew, remember I told you that you didn't have a daddy, like your cousins Angie and Sam and Michaela have?'

He nodded solemnly.

'Well…' She moistened her mouth and picked up a handful of bubbles, watching as they lay suspended there in the palm of her hand. 'Well, the thing is…'

The sound of the doorbell ringing stalled the rest of her sentence. She tossed the bubbles aside and quickly pulled the plug out of the bath and, scooping Matthew up in his towel, called out, 'Just a second.'

'Who is it, Mummy?' Matthew asked as Scarlett did her best to dry him as she walked to the front door of her flat. 'Are we having pizza again?'

'No, darling,' she said. 'It's not the pizza-delivery man. It's…it's…'

'A surprise?' he asked, with excitement building in his eyes. 'What sort of surprise?'

'Er…I'm not sure…it could be Mrs West. She might have run out of milk again.'

Scarlett opened the door, already knowing who it was, for she had felt it in every single cell of her body at the first sound of that bell.

Alessandro stood there, his eyes going immediately to the child wriggling in her arms. Such a rush of pain, panic and guilt passed through his body he felt as if he was not going to be able to keep upright. He tried to speak, but for some reason his throat refused to work. He swallowed half a dozen times but still nothing came out.

'Who is it, Mummy?' Matthew asked in a small-toddler sibilant whisper.

Scarlett looked at Alessandro with a direct and somewhat challenging look. 'This is your father, Matthew.'

Matthew wrinkled his brow and looked at her again. 'He's not dead, like Mrs West's cat Tinkles?'

'No, darling, he's not dead. He's very much alive.'

A silence measured the erratic pace of Alessandro's heart-beat before the little boy whispered up against his mother's ear, 'Can he speak?'

Scarlett smiled in spite of the tension of the moment, and when she looked at Alessandro his mouth, too, had tilted a fraction.

'Hello, Matthew,' Alessandro said, not knowing whether to offer his hand or bend down and kiss the child.

What did one do these days with small children?

He didn't know.

Over the years he'd actively avoided children of any age, knowing how much worse it made him feel about the decision he'd been forced to make.

'Hello…' the child said with a shy but totally engaging smile. 'Do you like cars?'

Alessandro felt a sharp pain begin in his abdomen and travel right through to his backbone, like a savage drill. 'Yes…yes, I love cars. I have several.'

The boy's eyes lit up, and Alessandro couldn't help noticing they were exactly the same colour as his, fringed with thick, sooty lashes.

'I've got twelve,' Matthew announced proudly.

'Twenteen?' Alessandro glanced at Scarlett with a quizzical look on his face.

'Twenty, darling,' she said, addressing the child. 'Remember how it goes after ten? Eleven, twelve, thirteen, fourteen—'

'Fifteen, sixteen, seventeen, eighteen, nineteen, twenty!' Matthew crowed.

'That is indeed a lot of cars,' Alessandro said, still struggling to hold himself together.

'Umm…perhaps you should come inside,' Scarlett said when she noticed a neighbour she didn't particularly like hovering in the stairwell.

'Thank you,' Alessandro said, stepped inside and closed the door.

Scarlett brushed a strand of her hair back with her one free hand. 'Umm…would you excuse us while I get Matthew into his pyjamas? He was in the bath when you rang the bell.'

'Sorry,' he said, looking uncharacteristically uncomfortable. 'Perhaps I should have phoned first.'

Scarlett wondered why he hadn't. But then, looking at him now, she realised he had probably needed time to gather himself. The news would no doubt have shocked him. He had clearly not expected to be proved wrong.

She felt for him, even as she felt angry that she had suffered alone for so long. It was a bewildering mix of emotions: resentment, regret, hate, love…

No she didn't love him any more, she decided. How could she? She had suffered too much as a result of his lack of trust. She wasn't going to allow herself to get caught out a second time.

'Can I wear my racing-car jammies?' Matthew asked as she carried him out of the small living-room.

'Sure you can,' she said. 'I washed them yesterday.'

'You won't tell Daddy I still sometimes wet the bed, will you Mummy?' he asked in another whisper, but his little voice carried regardless.

'No,' she said. 'Not if you don't want me to.'

Alessandro turned to look around the room, knowing it was pointless feeling shut out and angry. It was his fault for being so arrogantly confident. He should have at least given her the benefit of the doubt. He could have repeated the tests. He could even have checked the statistics on the internet like any other layman, for God's sake. He'd done it after he'd left the doctor's surgery, ashamed that he hadn't thought of it earlier.

It was all there. He'd even read of two pregnancies occurring five years after surgery.

He wondered how those two men had treated their partners. Had they cut them from their lives, accusing them of being unfaithful. Or had they stayed close, supporting them, and guiding them through what to all intents and purposes was an unplanned pregnancy.

It shocked him to the core that he hadn't once considered Scarlett's feelings about being pregnant at twenty-three. That was considered young these days, when most women got their career established before they thought about settling down. She had not only been young, but only just qualified as an interior designer. And he had thrown her out on the street, late at night in a foreign country, pregnant and alone.

No wonder she still hated him.

His eyes went to a photograph sitting on a side table and he picked it up and looked at it, emotion beginning to tighten his chest. It had obviously been taken the day she left hospital after the birth of Matthew. He could see the run-down outer-suburbs hospital building in the background.

Scarlett was holding him, a tiny bundle of blue in her arms, her still-swollen stomach visible, her breasts fuller than normal, and her gaze full of love as she looked down at the infant. But there was sadness in her smile. He could sense it.

You should have been there, the voice of accusation thundered in his brain. *You missed the birth of your child out of arrogance, ignorance and prejudice.*

Three whole years had passed.

He had not been there for a moment of his son's life. Not a single moment. He hadn't felt the first fluttery kicks in Scarlett's womb with his hand pressed against her abdomen. He hadn't been there for the first ultrasonic image of his son. He hadn't witnessed the moment of birth, heard that first mewing cry, had never been woken in the night by the howls of hunger that only an infant could perform with such fervour. He had missed everything, but he had no one to blame but himself.

Scarlett had faced it all alone, and how in the world he was going to make it up to her, or even to Matthew, was anyone's guess.

But he wanted to.

Oh, dear God, he wanted to—but there were several hurdles in the way.

The first one was to find out if Matthew was healthy. He certainly looked it; his limbs were strong and rounded with the plumpness of early childhood, his hair was glossy black, and his eyes clear and bright.

But Marco's had been too, until their world had been turned upside down…

CHAPTER TEN

SCARLETT tucked her son's night nappy out of sight under the elastic waist of his pyjamas and led him by the hand back out to the small living-room.

Alessandro was standing with his back to them, a photograph in his hands, and as he heard their footsteps he placed it back on the side table and faced them.

'Matthew would like to say goodnight,' Scarlett said, with a look he couldn't quite decipher.

He looked down at the child, the ache in his chest so unbearable he felt like he was going to cry, like he had done so uncontrollably at Marco's funeral.

'Can I call you Daddy?' Matthew asked, blinking up at him.

'Of course,' Alessandro said, squatting before him. 'But in Italy where I come from children call their father *Papa*. Can you say that?'

'*Papa*,' Matthew said with a dimpled grin. 'Is that right?'

Alessandro reached out and touched his child for the first time. He laid a hand on the boy's shoulder, but then, wanting more skin-on-skin contact, he placed his hand on the curve of his tiny cheek. 'That is perfect, my son,' he said, his voice breaking slightly over the words.

'Will you tuck me into bed and read me a story?' the little boy asked—and then, glancing briefly at his mother as if to ask her permission, added as he turned back, 'Mummy won't mind. She's always tired after work and she even skips a few pages. She thinks I don't notice, but I do.'

Alessandro smiled even though it hurt. Marco had been the same. He'd only had to hear a story once to have it memorised word for word. 'Sure, I would like to do that, very much,' he said. 'That is, if your mother does not mind.'

Scarlett met his gaze. 'No,' she said, trying but not quite managing to smile. 'I don't mind at all.'

A few minutes later Alessandro read a story about a wombat and an echidna, and how they managed to have a workable friendship in spite of their many differences.

He looked down after he had finished the second-last page, and saw the fan-like lashes of his son's eyes flutter a couple of times then close over his eyes, a soft sigh of total relaxation deflating his tiny chest, covered by a thin cotton sheet. In his hand was a tiny matchbox car, a black Maserati, the sight of which had affected Alessandro almost more than anything else so far.

He looked at that tiny chest moving up and down, and wondered if Scarlett had any idea of what could be lurking inside there, waiting like a time bomb to leap out in the future and cast a dark shadow over all of their lives.

When he came back out Scarlett was sitting with a magazine in her hands, her reading glasses perched on her nose, giving her that studious, intellectual look he had always found so incredibly sexy.

She looked up and removed her glasses. 'Is he asleep?'

'Yes,' he said, taking the sofa-chair opposite, a particularly uncomfortable one, he noticed. A spring of some sort was protruding into his left buttock, and he had to move a few times to avoid its insistent prong.

A silence threatened to halt all communication, but Alessandro had things to say and didn't want to let any more time pass. 'Is he well?' he asked somewhat abruptly.

She blinked a couple of times. 'Yes…mostly.'

He found himself leaning forward on the sofa, which activated the prodding spring once more. It made him realise how hard she had struggled to provide for their son. The irony of it was particularly heart-wrenching—she decorated penthouses worth millions, and yet she lived in a tiny cramped flat with furniture that looked like it had come out of a charity shop.

He cleared his throat, as if by doing so he could clear away his guilt, but it was pointless. It rose like a debris-ridden tide inside him, making his voice sound husky. 'What do you mean by "mostly"?' he asked.

'Alessandro, he's three years old.' Her tone was matter-of-fact. 'He's had numerous colds and stomach bugs. He's a little kid—they get sick all the time.'

'How sick?'

She frowned at the intensity of his gaze. 'Not enough to be hospitalised, although he came close once.'

He leaned forward even further. 'What happened on that occasion?'

Scarlett found his penetrating stare almost too much to cope with; she had to really fight to hold his gaze. 'He had a serious chest infection,' she said. 'He became wheezy, and it took a while for the antibiotics to kick in. The first lot the doctor prescribed gave Matthew an allergic reaction.'

'But he was not hospitalised?'

'No. I took a few days off work and treated him at home with an alternative antibiotic. He was fine in a week or so. It was a bad winter. Everyone went down with the same bug.'

'Is he particularly susceptible to chest infections?'

She chewed her lip as she thought about the other mothers she knew at crèche and what she knew of their children. 'No,' she answered at last. 'No more than the average child. Why are you asking such questions?'

He gave a little shrug, his expression giving nothing away. 'I have missed out on three years of his life. I am just trying to fill in the gaps.'

Her grey-blue gaze hardened as it met his. 'You could have been there from the first moment, but you chose to disbelieve me. I take it the doctor you saw confirmed my version of events?'

He let out a sigh that snagged at his throat like a mouthful of barbed wire. 'Yes. It has now been confirmed. It is rare, but it does occasionally happen. I have had a spontaneous rejoin of my *vas deferens*.'

'Do you need a DNA test to confirm Matthew as your son and not someone else's?'

Alessandro was ashamed to admit he had thought of it—but as soon as he had seen that child he had known he was his. A DNA test would only confirm what he already knew—Matthew was his son, the living breathing image of himself and his younger brother Marco, with all its harrowing burdens and consequences.

'No,' he said, not meeting her gaze. 'That will not be necessary. I have all the information I need.' *For now,* he added silently. A DNA test would have to be performed at some stage, but not the one she was thinking of.

Scarlett sat opposite him, trying to push her righteous anger to one side, but she couldn't quite manage it. She was secretly terrified he might take it upon himself to insist on regular access to Matthew.

Matthew had only known her as his chief care-giver. He hated being at crèche, in spite of the loving and well-trained staff, and on the few occasions Scarlett had been out at night the only people he liked babysitting him were Roxanne or her mother.

'Scarlett…' He pushed a hand through the black silk of his hair and met her gaze. 'I would like to discuss the role I want to play in Matthew's life now that I know he is mine.'

Here it comes, she thought, her stomach twisting and turning with dread. 'He's only three years old,' she said, sending him a flinty look. 'I hope you're not expecting him to fly back and forth like a parcel between Sydney and Milan several times a year? Because I won't allow it.'

A frown drew his brows together. 'I was not thinking of any such thing, not yet in any case. He is too young to be without his mother for one thing, and the other…'

Scarlett waited for him to continue, but instead he let out a sigh and got to his feet. She watched, her breath feeling as if she was drawing it into her lungs through a crushed drinking-straw, as he reached down and picked up the hospital photograph again. He stood looking down at it for endless seconds. His face side-on was like an expressionless mask, and yet she was almost certain she could see a film of moisture in his eyes as he put the frame back down and faced her fully.

'Tell me about him,' he said in a voice that didn't sound like his at all. 'Tell me everything.'

Scarlett wasn't sure where to begin. She didn't want to overload him with guilt, but neither did she want him to think it had been a breeze having his child without emotional and financial support. 'He's a lovely child,' she said. 'He was born at eleven in the morning and weighed seven pounds and three ounces. He's very advanced for his age; he walked at ten months, and spoke in full sentences at eighteen, which is unusual for boys; they are often slower with language. He loves cars, as you can see, and he loves animals. I wish I could have given him more than I have, but… Well, I gave him what I could when I could.'

'You did your best,' he said. 'I am amazed that you have achieved what you have while trying to raise a small child.'

'It wasn't always easy,' she admitted. 'But my mother has been down this road before, so I more or less knew what I was in for.'

Scarlett looked at his tortured expression. Seeing him finally accept Matthew as his son had been so incredibly poignant, it had moved her to tears. It would take him a few days, maybe even weeks, to realise the full extent of what he had missed out on in his son's life so far. He was so obviously affected by the realisation that he had made the biggest mistake of his life. He was doing his best to find a way to make amends, but how that was going to impact on her and Matthew remained to be seen.

'I want an active role in his life,' Alessandro said. 'I know it will be hard for you to accept, but I want to be a real father to him now.'

She didn't answer, just stood there before him with uncertainty and fear in her gaze. And no wonder, Alessandro thought. He still found it hard to believe just a thin wall of plasterboard separated him from the sleeping form of his son. The son he had betrayed by being so adamant Scarlett had lied to him.

Three years of Matthew's life had gone past, each and

every day containing a thousand memories that he would never have access to. It was gone for ever; the babyhood of the only child he would ever have was gone.

His eyes went to the photograph again. It was like a magnet. Every time he tried to avert his gaze, it tracked back to that small rectangle of truth as if pulled by powerful strings.

He should have been standing there beside her with a smile as wide as any proud father's. Instead he had been several-thousand kilometres away, seething with hatred.

But now he was here, and he had to do something about preparing Scarlett for the burden of knowledge that had deadened his soul for so long. She would surely be devastated to find out Matthew could have a life-threatening condition. What parent wouldn't be?

He let another silence pass for a moment or two.

'I was thinking we could get married as soon as possible,' he finally said.

Her eyes bulged with shock, or was it anger? He couldn't quite tell. *'Excuse me?'* she said, her mouth so tight it looked like it had been stitched into place. 'What did you say?'

He cleared his throat. 'I said I thought we could get married.'

'For what reason?'

He didn't like the sound of her tone, or the contentious look she was firing his way, but he soldiered on regardless. 'We have a son,' he said. 'He has a mother, but he has not had a father for the first three years of his life. I am prepared to step into that role and do what I can to make it up to him.'

'You can *never* make it up to him,' she said, her eyes flashing with venom as they hit his. 'You have your evidence now, but where were you when he and I really needed you? How dare you think you can waltz back into our lives on the basis of a pathology test and suddenly become father of the year?'

'I have some rights, surely?' he argued, even though he understood her position. 'I know I did not plan for this to happen, but it has, and I am prepared to face the consequences.'

She threw him a blistering look. 'I don't want to marry you. You're only asking me because of Matthew. How do you think that makes me feel?'

'Your feelings or even mine do not come into it,' he said. 'I am trying to do what is best for our child.'

'You seem to have forgotten something,' she said with a glittering glare. 'I hate you for what you did to me, Alessandro.'

'I hope to God you have not communicated that to my son,' he inserted into the taut silence.

Scarlett wasn't entirely sure what she had been expecting him to say in response, but it certainly hadn't been that. He seemed to be genuinely concerned about Matthew. It made her feel ashamed that she hadn't factored in her little boy's feelings and needs in this most complicated of situations.

'No…' she said on an expelled breath. 'Of course not.'

'But you told him I was dead.'

Her head came up, her eyes reluctantly meeting his. 'Yes. I thought it was the best thing all round. My mother was deserted by my father before I was born. She struggled so hard to provide for my sister and me. I knew I couldn't come home and announce I was pregnant to a man who refused to acknowledge my baby's existence. I was so distraught, I found myself telling Mum and Sophie the father had been killed in a road accident. It seemed believable.'

'Did you tell *anyone* the truth?'

She shook her head and looked down at her hands. 'Not until the other day when you came into the studio. Before that I was tempted to many times, to Roxanne mostly, but I didn't see the point. You had denied all responsibility. I didn't see that changing any time soon.'

He sent a hand on a rough pathway through his hair again, making it stick up at odd angles. 'If only you had sent me a photo or two,' he said heavily. 'I would have had no choice but to sit up and take notice.'

She lifted her gaze back to his. 'So now it's my fault for not pressing the issue a bit harder, is it?'

Alessandro jerked back as if she had struck him. 'No, I am not saying that. I just wish…' He didn't finish the sentence. He couldn't think of the words to say. He wished he could rewrite the past. He wished he could have told Scarlett four years ago of his love for her, but the burden that was attached to that love had prevented him. He wished he could tell her now of how worried he was that her world, her relatively secure world, could come crashing down at any moment.

And it was *his* fault.

Scarlett swung away in despair. 'I can't believe you have the audacity to come here and expect me to fall into your plans as if the last four years haven't happened.'

'I understand your reluctance, but I am thinking about our son. He deserves better than this.'

She spun back to glare at him. 'What do you mean, "he deserves better than this"? Are you somehow suggesting I'm not doing a proper job of raising him?'

He gave the room a sweeping glance before returning his gaze to her combative one. 'This is a small flat. It is up three flights of stairs, and as far as I can tell has no air-conditioning. It is not the place for a young child.'

'The air-conditioning broke down a couple of weeks ago,' she said. 'The landlord hasn't got around to fixing it yet. And, besides, I can't afford to rent a house with a garden as much as I'd like to. I have bills enough as it is, trying to run a business.'

'I will take care of all of your expenses, Scarlett,' he said. 'I will pay off any of your loans and credit cards. I will also arrange for Matthew's name to be put down at the school you would like him to attend when he is of age.'

She gave him a narrowed-eyed look, her tone deliberately sarcastic. 'Forgive me if I'm wrong, but I can sense a list of conditions attached to that very generous offer?'

His eyes glinted with determination. 'Just the one, actually,' he said. 'Marriage to me.'

'No.' She clamped her lips tight over the word.

'Do not make me resort to more forceful means, Scarlett,' he said, with rising frustration. 'I am trying my best to be patient and understanding with you. We once had a good relationship. We could work towards having one again for Matthew's sake.'

Scarlett threw him a scornful look. 'You think by just walking in here and offering marriage everything is going to magically turn out right? What planet have you been living on? We hate each other, Alessandro. I don't see that changing just by shoving a wedding band on our hands and smiling for the cameras.'

'I realise you have every reason to hate me,' he said. 'But for Matthew's sake I must ask you to please try and control those feelings. I do not want him to grow up in a hostile environment.'

'I'm *not* marrying you.'

'You are only saying that because you want to punish me.'

She rolled her eyes at him. 'No, I'm saying it because it's actually true. I apologise if your ego finds it a little hard to accept—but, thanks but no thanks, as the saying goes.'

He stepped towards her and took her by the upper arms in a hold that was on the surface gentle, but Scarlett could feel the steely strength of his fingers the moment she tried to pull away.

'Listen to me, Scarlett,' he ground out, his eyes locking on hers. 'You will marry me or I will close your business down. You will be begging on the streets for your next meal, I guarantee it.'

Her eyes flashed with hatred. 'If you ruin me you'll be ruining your own son. What sort of man are you?'

'I have the sort of legal connections that will ensure I gain full custody of Matthew,' he said, his voice hard and determined. 'You will see him only if and when I say you can.'

Scarlett felt the cold, hard stone of despair land in her stomach, the weight of it threatening to send her insides to the floor at her feet.

She had underestimated him.

He had the sort of money to do anything he wanted. If he took it upon himself to ruin her, he could do it. If he wanted full custody of Matthew, he would and could get it. The only way she could stop him would be to do what he wanted her to do.

But marrying a man she had once loved with all her heart, only to have been rejected so cruelly and unfairly, was more than she could bear. Her anger towards him had festered for close to four years. It was like a hard nut deep inside her that wouldn't dissolve. If she allowed herself to be coerced into a loveless marriage, what damage would it do to her? Not to mention Matthew, who would surely sense the enmity between his parents. He was a deeply sensitive and highly intelligent child; it would gradually erode his self-esteem to find his parents were only together for the sake of appearances.

She slowly dragged her tortured gaze back to his. 'Don't make me do this, Alessandro. Do you really want me to hate you more than I already do?'

His eyes were more brown than green as they held hers. 'It is a strange sort of hate, don't you think? Your eyes burn with it, and yet your body burns with something else.'

Scarlett became increasingly aware of the heat of his body against hers and the warmth of his breath as it caressed her face. She nervously moistened her lips, tasting wine and temptation as his mouth slowly but inexorably lowered towards hers.

The first touch of his lips against hers was like an explosion of flammable materials. The blood thrummed in her ears as she felt the sensual glide of his tongue against the seam of her mouth, not asking but demanding entry.

She gave it without hesitation, her lips opening on a deep sigh of pleasure as his tongue invaded her mouth, sweeping and stroking and thrusting against hers with earth-shattering expertise. She felt as if she was on fire. Her whole body was leaping to life; her breasts became heavy and tingly, her legs loosened, her spine melted, and her arms moved to his chest, her fingers splayed at first, then clutching at him as his kiss became even more intensely sexual.

He nipped at her bottom lip in a teasing manner and she responded by doing the same, but a little harder. He groaned deep at the back of his throat and nipped again, his tongue sweeping over the indentation of where his teeth had been. She bit him again, but softer this time, sucking on him, tugging on him until he took control again, his tongue playing with hers in a teasing come-and-get-me manner.

Scarlett knew she had to put a stop to this before she melted into a pool at his feet. She could already feel the dew of desire between her legs, the throbbing pulse building to fever pitch until she could barely stand.

She pulled out of his embrace—obviously catching him off-guard, for otherwise she knew he would not have released her until he was ready to do so.

She stood, desperately trying to get her breathing back under control, her lips tingling as if a thousand electrodes were attached while her heart thudded haphazardly. 'You sh-shouldn't have done that,' she said, annoyed that her voice sounded so breathless and uneven.

His eyes still burned with desire as they held hers. 'Why not?' he asked.

She glared at him. 'You know why.'

'As of three days ago we were already involved, so I do not see the problem.'

'I was only involved with you as I had no choice. You practically blackmailed me into your bed.'

'It did not take too much pressure to get you there,' he said. 'It makes me wonder just how many other men have been in your life since we broke up.'

Scarlett felt like slapping him, but then she realised she was just as angry at herself. As he had pointed out, she hadn't really put up much resistance, which didn't give her much moral high-ground to stand on. 'I know you'll find this hard to believe, but there's been no one since you,' she said.

'What about Kirby?'

'I have never been involved with Dylan,' she said. 'He's always been like a brother to me.'

His brow was creased in a frown. 'So there has been no one?'

'No. Being a single mother makes dating difficult. You have to be so careful these days with whom you allow your child to have contact. I decided it was too much effort.' She sent him brittle glance and added, 'It's probably hard for a man like you to understand, but I never once considered getting rid of him.'

Alessandro met her flashing eyes and inwardly sighed. One of the reasons he'd had a vasectomy was to prevent any lover of his having to face such an agonising decision.

'Was it a difficult pregnancy?' he asked after a little pause.

She took her time answering, her bottom lip suffering a little nibble by her teeth before she released it in order to speak. 'It was hard being alone. I wanted to share the whole experience with…with someone, but that wasn't possible.'

'If only I had known back then what I know now,' he mused.

Her expression instantly hardened. 'You no doubt would have insisted I have a termination, wouldn't you? The last thing you wanted to be was tied down with a wife and a child. You've said it several times since. You lived the life of a playboy when I met you, and still do; I always suspected I was nothing more than a temporary diversion, for if I had been anything else you would never have doubted me.'

'I cannot change the past any more than you can, Scarlett,' he said. 'We have a son who needs both his parents. Marriage is our only option. I will not settle for anything less.'

Scarlett didn't bother hiding her contempt. 'You weren't so keen on marriage and babies a few days ago.'

His hazel eyes darkened as they clashed with hers. 'There will be no other babies. I want you to be clear on that right from the start.'

There was a taut silence.

'What if I am already pregnant?' she asked.

A tiny jackhammer seemed to be at work beneath his skin at the side of his mouth, which was pulled tight. 'Are you saying you are not on the Pill?'

'Why would I be?' she asked. 'As I told you—I haven't slept with anyone since you.'

He swung away from her, his expression clouding with something she couldn't quite identify. She watched as he paced the room back and forth, his long strides having to shorten considerably to fit between the sofa and the shabby wall-unit.

When he finally turned back to look at her his face was ashen. 'If it has happened…' he swallowed deeply '…then we will deal with it. How soon will you know?'

She chewed at the inside of her mouth, trying to recall where she was in her cycle. 'I'm due in a few days,' she said, not able to meet his eyes.

'I have organised to have the procedure redone,' he said. 'I'm going to hospital as a day case.'

Scarlett felt as if she had been struck by something heavy and blunt deep and low in her abdomen. 'You're asking too much, Alessandro,' she said, lifting her gaze back to his. 'I want another child. I don't want Matthew to grow up without a brother or sister.'

His jaw was set in intractable lines. 'Well, I do not want another child. I did not want the one I have, but there is nothing I can do about it now.'

She glared at him in outrage. 'How can you *say* that? Matthew is a living, breathing child. He's the most precious little person. He's your flesh and blood, for God's sake. He's already halfway to loving you.'

He raked a hand through his hair and turned away on a

rough sigh. 'Yes…yes, I know, but I did not intend to pass on my flesh and blood…to anyone. I thought I had done everything possible to prevent it, but somehow…'

'Why, Alessandro?' Her voice came out as a hoarse whisper. 'Why are you so determined about this?'

'I do not want to inflict suffering on anyone, and least of all a child.'

'But how will you do that?' she asked, her brow wrinkled in bewilderment. 'You have so much to offer a child.'

'I have nothing but money,' he said, turning to face her again. 'Believe me, it is not nearly enough.'

Scarlett frowned as she looked at the flicker of pain come and go in his eyes. 'Money isn't important, it's love that counts.'

His mouth slanted mockingly. 'There you go using that four-letter word again.'

'I don't want to marry a man who isn't capable of love,' she said. 'What sort of father will you be if you can't even express love to your wife and child? It's not normal.'

'When we marry you will be my wife in every sense of the word, Scarlett, so that will make it very normal—very normal indeed.'

'What if I don't agree?' she said, lifting her chin a fraction.

His jaw became even more rigid. 'You know I have the power to do what I threatened to do.'

'Yes, and the lack of morality to do it,' she threw back. 'I can't bear the thought of being tied to you indefinitely. I can't think of anything worse.'

There was a heartbeat or two of silence.

'I do not recall saying we will remain married indefinitely,' he said.

Scarlett felt the wind drop right out of her self-righteous

sails. She stood for a moment, trying not to show how his statement had affected her. But even so she felt her teeth sink into her bottom lip again before she could stop them, and this time she tasted blood.

'I want Matthew to legally bear my name,' he said. 'The best way he can do that is for you to marry me. The marriage will continue for as long as I feel it is necessary.'

'Necessary for what?' she asked, her heart skipping all over the place.

His eyes were unreadable as they held hers. 'I will meet you tomorrow at the old Arlington Hotel building at ten a.m. to discuss the arrangements. In the meantime, I will deposit funds in your bank account which should see to your business loan and any other outstanding debts you might have.'

Scarlett watched as he opened the door to leave, the words of protest stuck—along with her tongue—to the roof of her mouth.

He turned back from the door to look at her. 'Do not think of rejecting my offer of marriage, Scarlett,' he added. 'It would not be in Matthew's interests if you did.'

'And what about *my* interests?' she asked. 'Have those been factored in somewhere in your scheme of playing temporary happy-families?'

A shutter seemed to come down over his brown-green gaze. 'I am doing my level best to make up for what you have suffered,' he said in a deep, gravelly tone. 'I made a mistake that I will probably regret for the rest of my life.'

'You're about to make another one,' she said. 'Marrying me is not going to solve anything—if anything it's going to make things worse.'

'You will be well rewarded for your efforts.'

She glared at him. 'Don't insult me by offering me disgusting amounts of money—or is that how you usually buy female affection these days?'

His expression barely changed, but Scarlett saw the way his knuckles turned to white beneath his tan as he gripped the door knob. 'I will see you tomorrow,' he said in a deceptively even tone. 'If you do not turn up, then I will have no choice but to assume you are not only putting your business on the line but your son as well.'

Scarlett wanted the last word but he closed the door before she could even think of it, much less get it past the knot of tension in her throat. She whooshed out a breath and sagged against the nearest flat surface, and closed her eyes as she heard the rumble and roar of his car as it left.

CHAPTER ELEVEN

'I CAN'T believe you lied to us for all these years,' Scarlett's sister Sophie said over the phone later that evening. 'I don't know what I'm going to say to Hugh when he gets home. I saw that article in the paper and immediately called Mum. What on earth were you thinking?'

Scarlett sent her eyes heavenwards. 'This is not about you, Sophie.'

'Of course it's about me!' her sister railed. 'Hugh and I are high-profile people. I have told everyone for years that you are a grief-stricken single mother, and now I find out you've been lying about your child's father. I feel *so* betrayed.'

Scarlett felt like grinding her teeth, but only stopped because her sister had acute hearing for that sort of thing, being married to a cosmetic dentist. 'I didn't mean to hurt you, but I was trying to do what I thought was the best—'

'When can we meet him?' Sophie cut her off. 'What about tomorrow night? I can get our housekeeper to make a special meal.'

'Alessandro's a very busy man,' Scarlett said. 'He won't have time to traipse around meeting all my relatives.'

'They will be *his* relatives once you are married,' Sophie pointed out.

'Ahem.' Scarlett pointedly cleared her throat. 'I haven't exactly said I was going to marry him.'

'For God's sake, Scarlett, he's your son's father!' Sophie cried. 'You have to marry him. Or hasn't he asked you?'

'Yes, he has, but I don't like the conditions.'

'Listen, Scarlett, when you're marrying a billionaire you don't think about the conditions,' Sophie said with typical older-sister pragmatism. 'Even if the marriage only lasts a year or two you'll be set for life.'

'I don't want to be set for life, I want to be happy.'

'Do you feel anything for him?' Sophie asked.

Scarlett rolled her lips together as she thought about it. 'Yes, but I don't think it's the best way to start a marriage.'

'What is that supposed to mean?'

'It means I'm not sure what I feel about him,' Scarlett answered. 'He's Matthew's father, so I can't exactly hate him, but I don't want to feel what I felt for him before.'

'You don't have to love him to marry him,' Sophie said. 'Plenty of marriages survive on much less.'

Scarlett couldn't help feeling her sister was talking from experience. Sophie had always been very determined about her life plan. She'd had a checklist from the age of fifteen, and any man who hadn't got a tick in all the boxes had been summarily dismissed as potential husband-material.

Hugh Gallagher was the first one who'd come along who had met all her demands, but Scarlett often wondered if her sister had sold herself short. At the time of night when most secure couples would be cuddling up in bed, Sophie rang to chat about nothing and everything. And every time Scarlett asked where Hugh was, her sister would answer somewhat dismissively that he was operating on a private patient.

Scarlett felt like asking just how many wisdom teeth there were in Sydney to be taken out at close to ten p.m.

'What does Matthew think of him?' Sophie asked.

'I'm not sure he's old enough to really understand what's going on,' Scarlett said. 'But he seemed to really enjoy having him here this evening.'

'When are you going to see Alessandro again?'

'Tomorrow,' Scarlett answered with another flutter of unease in her belly. 'We're meeting to go over the designs I've been working on.'

'Wow, that's going to be quite a feather in your cap,' Sophie said. 'I read about it in the weekend supplement. The new Marciano Palazzo hotel is going to be one of the most luxurious Sydney has ever seen.'

'Yes, I know.'

'Don't blow this chance, Scarlett,' Sophie said. 'This is an opportunity of a lifetime. Think of what he could give Matthew.'

Scarlett tightened her mouth. 'I just want him to love him, that's all.'

'What about you?' Sophie asked. 'Do you want him to love you too?'

Scarlett released a long sigh. 'That's every girl's dream, isn't it?'

'Yes, but sometimes love is not enough.'

'You're starting to sound like Alessandro,' Scarlett said. 'He's as cynical as they come, but I still don't really know why.'

'He'll tell you when he's ready,' her sister said. 'It's a guy thing. They hate revealing their vulnerability.'

'I have never seen Alessandro as someone who would

allow himself to be vulnerable. He likes to be in control at all times and in all places.'

'Then you'll have to stick by him until he feels safe enough to do so,' Sophie said. 'This would have knocked him for six, I imagine, finding out he'd fathered a child he had no intention of ever fathering.'

'I know,' Scarlett said, looking at the photograph that had transfixed Alessandro so much while he had been there. 'I realise how hard it is for him, but I have had close to four years of dealing with this alone. I'm not quite ready to forgive him.'

'You don't have to forgive him, just marry him, and let the rest take care of itself,' Sophie advised. 'It's really the only thing you can do.'

'He doesn't want another child.'

'Oh… Well, then, I guess you'll have to accept that. Remember how hard it was for Mum? I swore I'd never let it happen to me, and I haven't. You need to grab this chance while you've got it. If you keep him dangling too long he might withdraw the offer.'

'Alessandro doesn't *offer*,' Scarlett said with a little scowl. 'He demands.'

'Marry him, Scarlett,' Sophie said. 'He deserves a chance to put things right. You never know, he might even fall in love with you this time around.'

'Yeah, right, as if that's going to happen,' Scarlett said as she hung up the phone a minute or two later.

Scarlett caught sight of Alessandro's striking figure as soon as the Arlington came into view. He was wearing a hard hat, standing beside a much shorter man who was similarly attired, and who she assumed was one of the engineers he had employed. They had their heads together over some plans, but

Alessandro looked up as if he had felt her presence, his eyes locking with hers.

'Good morning, *cara*,' he said, removing his hat to bend down to brush a brief, hard kiss to her mouth before she could counteract it. 'Barry, this is my fiancée, Scarlett Fitzpatrick. Scarlett, this is Barry Alder, my chief engineer.'

For the sake of politeness Scarlett had no choice but to shake the other man's hand, although the glare she sent Alessandro's way threatened to save the painters the job of stripping the old paint off the walls. 'Pleased to meet you,' she said, stretching her mouth into a stiff little smile.

Barry Alder took off his hard hat and smiled back. 'I saw the announcement in the paper this morning. Alessandro is a lucky man. Congratulations on your engagement.'

Scarlett felt her stomach drop. 'Umm…thank you.'

Alessandro handed the engineer his hat as he put an arm around Scarlett's waist and drew her into his side. 'We will leave you to it, Barry. I am taking Scarlett out to choose an engagement ring. Call me if there is anything you need.'

'It all looks pretty straightforward,' Barry said. 'The foundations are fine. I'll get back to you on those quotes about the footbridge. It shouldn't take more than a day or so.'

'No hurry,' Alessandro said. 'I have other things on my mind right now.'

Scarlett waited until the engineer had moved on before spinning out of Alessandro's hold. 'What the hell is going on?' she asked with a glittering glare. 'I don't recall saying I was going to marry you.'

He captured one of her hands with his and tugged her closer. 'You do not have any choice, *cara*. I thought you understood that.'

'I have no intention of marrying you. I don't care how

many press releases you make to the contrary, I am *not* going to bow to your commands as if I have no mind of my own.'

'You have a choice,' he said smoothly. 'You either marry me or you lose your business and your son.'

'You can't do that,' she said, but she knew he could and would if pressed to do so.

His eyes hardened as they clashed with hers. 'You think you can take me on in a legal battle, Scarlett? You do not have a chance. You are foolish to even consider taking me on in a battle of wills. I will always win.'

'You have lost three years of your son's life because of your arrogant confidence,' she threw back. 'How much else are you prepared to lose?'

He held her defiant look for a lengthy moment. 'We will be working and living together in a matter of a week,' he said. 'It would be advisable to get any ill feeling out of the way now.'

'It's going to take me decades, much less weeks, to forgive you.'

'I am not asking you to forgive me,' he said. 'In fact, I am not asking you to do anything. I am *telling* you what is going to happen and when it will happen. We will be married in a week's time. I have organised a special licence. You and Matthew will move into my house in Double Bay tomorrow, and from that moment we will live as man and wife.'

'I am *not* going to sleep with you.'

A hint of a smile lurked at the edges of his mouth. 'It took me three days to get you into bed four years ago, and less than that the second time around,' he said. 'Do not lock yourself into any tight corners, *cara*. You know you will have to back down eventually. It is the way things are between us.'

Scarlett felt her face heating with shame at how she had

responded to him so unrestrainedly. There wasn't a part of her that hadn't been affected by him. Even now she could feel her pulse racing, and her breathing becoming shallow and uneven in his disturbing presence.

'Where is Matthew?' he asked.

'He's at crèche. I pick him up at five-thirty.'

He frowned. 'Isn't that rather a long day for a small child to be in care?'

'I don't have any other choice,' she said with a stinging glare. 'I can't afford a nanny.'

'I can arrange a nanny for you. Even a few hours a week would surely help? The rest of the time I would like to spend with him. I need to establish my relationship with him.'

'You can't rush things with a small child,' she said. 'He needs time to understand you are his father. It's a big thing for him.'

'It is a very big thing for me,' he said and, raking a hand through his hair, added, 'God knows I am still trying to come to terms with it.'

'Well, bully for you,' she said with a curl of her lip. 'You're the one who wouldn't believe me when I told you I was expecting him.'

Alessandro looked down at her grey-blue gaze that was burning with resentment, wondering if he should tell her why he had so desperately avoided becoming a father. But then he recalled the devastation on his mother's face the day Marco had been diagnosed. It wouldn't be fair to dump that burden on Scarlett in the middle of a busy city-street with the noise of jackhammers and traffic going on in the background. He would have to prepare her carefully for the shock of her life. He wasn't sure how he was going to do it, but it would have to be done, and sooner rather than later.

'I cannot change how I reacted back then, Scarlett. If I could turn back the clock, I would, but we have to move on now for Matthew's sake. I want to be a father to him, a real father in every sense of the word, and the only way I can do that is to be your husband.'

'Even though you don't love me?' she asked with a sudden film of moisture shining in her eyes.

He reached out with the pad of his thumb, stalled the progress of the first tear that escaped and blotted it gently against her cheekbone. 'I am willing to learn how to be a good father, *cara*, so who knows?'

Scarlett drew in a scratchy breath as he led her away from the dust and debris of the building site, the hard edges of her anger softening so much she felt as if she was melting from the inside out.

She *wanted* to be angry with him.

She *needed* to be angry with him to stop herself from…

She gave herself a brisk mental shake and strode along the uneven pavement alongside him, her head down in fierce concentration. She wasn't even going to think about loving him again. He didn't deserve it for not trusting her.

But even so, when his arm came out like a barrier to prevent her stepping in front of a turning car, Scarlett felt a tremor of awareness rumble through her being as his gaze briefly engaged hers. She looked up into the depths of his eyes and felt another layer of anger peel away until all she had left was her unprotected heart, aching for what might never come to pass….

Although it had not been her intention to simply go along with his plans, Scarlett found herself just minutes later sitting in an exclusive jeweller's shop with an exquisite diamond on her finger.

'Do you like it?' Alessandro asked, his hand gentle and protective on her shoulder.

'Yes, but—'

'We will take it,' he said to the jeweller. 'And the wedding rings as well.'

Scarlett watched as he signed the credit-card slip with a quick, dark slash of his signature, her stomach caving in when she turned to see the media already gathered outside to have the first photograph and interview. TV cameras were being angled at her, big fluffy microphones poised for when she and Alessandro walked into the hot summer sunshine.

'Do not worry, *tesore mio*,' Alessandro said as he drew her to her feet, his arm going about her waist. 'I will handle the press. Just smile and look happy.'

'Mr Marciano.' One of the three television interviewers got in first. 'Congratulations on your engagement to Scarlett Fitzpatrick. Does this mean you will be staying longer in Sydney than you had originally planned?'

'But of course,' Alessandro said, smiling politely.

Scarlett listened as a volley of questions and short, impersonal answers flew back and forth until an older rather, forceful-looking female journalist jostled forward with her microphone.

'Is it true, Mr Marciano, that Scarlett Fitzpatrick is the mother of your three-year-old son?' she asked. 'A son you had not even known existed until a week ago?'

Scarlett felt the tension in Alessandro's body as he stood beside her with his arm encircling her waist. 'Yes, she is,' he said in a clipped tone. 'Now, if you will excuse us, we have to—'

'Do you have any comment to make on the current medical condition of your son, Mr Marciano?' the journalist persisted.

Scarlett glanced up at Alessandro in confusion but his expression was inscrutably tight. 'No, I do not have any comment to make, other than he is a very healthy little boy,' he said. 'Now, if you will please make way—'

'Miss Fitzpatrick.' The journalist shifted targets with consummate ease. 'You must be very relieved to have your little son declared healthy. Were you worried he might also be a carrier?'

Scarlett felt the colour drain out of her face, and her chest suddenly felt as if someone very heavy had just sat upon it, crushing her lungs so she couldn't draw in a breath. 'Umm…a c-carrier?' she stammered, glancing up at Alessandro for help but his features were stonier than a statue.

She turned back to the journalist, her heart beginning to hit and miss a few beats. 'A carrier of…of what?'

CHAPTER TWELVE

'I WAS going to tell you,' Alessandro said as he bundled her into his car a few tense minutes later, his expression still looking as if it had been carved from granite.

Scarlett was opening and closing her mouth, as she had been doing ever since he had dragged her away from the press, her chest still so tight she could barely breathe, let alone get a word out.

The journalist hadn't minced any words. It seemed the older woman had found out a whole lot more about Alessandro Marciano's background than the young woman who had loved him and given birth to his son.

Still loved him, Scarlett corrected herself. She had been fooling herself into believing otherwise, but there was no point denying it now.

'I just did not want to dump it on you like that bitch of a journalist just did,' he said through gritted teeth as he started the car with a roar. 'I wanted to prepare you for the possibility that Matthew might have cystic fibrosis like my brother Marco, or if not he could—like me—be a carrier.'

Scarlett looked down at her still-shaking hands. The news had totally stunned her. She had not expected anything like this. She had believed Alessandro to be a playboy by choice, a man who actively sought no strings in his relationships for selfish reasons. She had never once thought there could be some other explanation. She couldn't begin to imagine how he had suffered and agonised over his decision to become sterilised, especially at so young an age.

The loss of his younger brother had clearly devastated him. In the whole time she had known him he had not once uttered a word about having a sibling, let alone having lost him to the debilitating and all-too-often ultimately fatal respiratory illness.

'My brother was three and a half years old when he was diagnosed,' Alessandro said into the silence. 'He had been more or less healthy until that point. He had the occasional chest infection, but things went downhill from there. He spent most of his childhood in hospital, and when he was not in hospital he was being pummelled by physiotherapists at home trying to clear his lungs.'

'I'm so sorry…' Her voice came out as a broken whisper. 'I am *so* sorry…'

'You have nothing to be sorry for,' he said. 'I should have told you earlier. I have not spoken of Marco's death for many years to anyone, not even my parents. It still upsets them both so much. Marco lost his childhood due to his illness and his future due to his death. He spent every day suffering while I looked on helplessly.'

Scarlett wanted to reach out to him and hold him close but he was concentrating on negotiating his way through the thick city traffic.

'I would have gladly changed places with him,' he continued in the same ragged tone. 'I felt so damned guilty for being the healthy one. When the doctors suggested genetic testing, I felt marginally better to find out that I had not exactly escaped. I was a carrier.'

'Is that why you…?'

He didn't wait for her to even frame the rest of her question. 'Yes. I decided I was not going to take any chances. Although both parents need to be a carrier to produce a child with cystic fibrosis, I was not prepared to risk it. I had seen enough. Neither of my parents knew they were carriers until Marco was diagnosed. Their marriage which had been steady enough to that point fell apart. They each wanted to blame the other. They *still* blame each other.'

'But it's no one's fault,' she said. 'How can it be anyone's fault? It's just the way the dice fall.'

He let out a long, uneven sigh. 'I know, but I can also understand how each of them feels. It is hard when you carry the genetic blueprint for a disease. You just want to get rid of it from your life, to pretend it is not there.'

'And the only way you could do that was to remove any chance of becoming a father,' she said, beginning to chew at her lip.

'Yes,' he said, flicking a quick, shadowed glance her way. 'But now I *am* a father.'

Scarlett prayed fervently that her gut feeling was right on this, even though the hammer of doubt began to pound inside her brain with deafening force. 'I don't think Matthew has it, Alessandro. He's fine. He's a healthy little boy.'

His hands tightened on the steering wheel. 'How can you be sure?' he asked. 'He will have to be tested. Even if he does not develop the disease, he could be a carrier. Either way we have to have the test done so we will know what we are dealing with.'

'Is that why you are insisting on marrying me?' she asked after a short pause.

He didn't answer immediately, but Scarlett couldn't tell if that was because the car in front had just done an illegal manoeuvre which Alessandro had to quickly counteract, or whether he was still thinking about how to respond. 'Marriage is our only option,' he finally said. 'It will give Matthew my name, which is important to me for legal reasons. He is and will remain my only heir.'

Scarlett surreptitiously pressed her hands against her flat stomach. They had made love without protection. He had assumed as he had four years ago that he wouldn't need it—however she…

'I am sorry you had to hear it the way you did,' he said. 'I would have given anything to spare you that.'

She reached out a hand, laid it on his thigh and gently squeezed. 'It's all right, Alessandro,' she said softly. 'I understand your reluctance to tell me sooner, I really do.'

He picked up her hand, brought it up to his mouth and held it tightly against his lips so she felt the movement of each agonised word against her skin as he spoke. 'I do not want to lose him, Scarlett. I have only just realised he is mine. I have already missed three years of his life. I could not bear to lose him again now.'

She fought back tears as he released her hand. 'I won't let that happen,' she said, gripping both hands tightly in her lap. 'Nothing and no one is going to take my son off me. *Nothing.*'

He gave her a bleak look as he turned into his driveway. 'You sound exactly like my mother,' he said as he activated the remote control on the gates. 'But, when she should have been celebrating Marco's coming of age, she was preparing for his funeral instead. He died the day before his eighteenth birthday. She has never quite recovered from it, nor has my father.'

'I'm sorry,' she said again.

'We will have lunch together, and then I want to collect Matthew and spend the afternoon and evening with him. I have organised for the doctor to come to your flat to take some blood for testing. I thought it would be less stressful for Matthew than taking him to the surgery. Is that all right with you?'

'Of course,' she said, moistening her dry lips, her heart beginning to thud again with dread. 'Yes, of course it is.'

He came around to open her door and as she got out he kept her hand in his and brought her up close. 'We will marry at the end of the week. I know it is short notice, but I do not want to waste any more time.'

She tried to get her hand back but he held it firm. 'Surely we don't have to rush things?'

'I know how you feel, but I do not want the press to go on and on with this. Believe me, they will hound us relentlessly. It is a matter of personal privacy. Also, I do not want to miss another moment of my son's life. I want him under my roof and under my protection. My parents will want to fly out to meet Matthew, but I will not have them come here until the media attention dies down. It will be best if we marry quickly and get on with our lives so that we are left alone.'

Scarlett could understand his position, but she felt as if things had escalated out of her control. Just a couple of hours ago she had been adamant that she was not going to be railroaded into marriage with him, but now…

She looked at him covertly as he led the way into his house, his face now devoid of the heart-wrenching emotion she knew was lying just under the surface. He was a deep and complex man, nothing like the arrogant self-serving playboy she had made him out to be. He was responsible and caring, and deeply hurt by the cruel hand of fate.

He turned to look at her as he pushed open the door for her to precede him. 'He looks like him,' he said, his voice sounding rough and uneven.

She felt her stomach clench. 'Matthew looks like Marco?'

'Yes.' His broad shoulders went down in a sigh as he closed the door and leaned back against it. 'If I hadn't seen your computer screen-saver the other day I would still be insisting he could not possibly be my son.'

She went to him then, hugging him around the waist, her head buried against his chest. 'At least you know now,' she said huskily. 'That's all that matters.'

Alessandro bent his chin to the top of her head and breathed in the summer-jasmine fragrance of her hair. 'Yes,' he said, his heart feeling like a lead weight in his chest. 'I know now.'

'Mummy!' Matthew said gleefully, and then when he saw the tall figure two steps behind added with even more excitement, 'Papa!'

Alessandro scooped up his son and held him close. The tiny but strong limbs clutching at him reassured him just as much as they tortured him with guilt. 'How was your day?' he asked.

'Good. I made a special thing for you.'

'Oh really?' Alessandro asked, looking a little bewildered.

'Box work,' Scarlett said in an undertone, pointing to the cardboard boxes and other craft materials on the small tables scattered about the room. 'He made a jewellery box for me the other day. It's bright green, with pipe cleaners for handles.'

'Oh.'

Matthew came over with a proud smile and handed his

father a teetering assortment of small cardboard-cartons and yogurt containers pasted together rather haphazardly.

'Wow,' Alessandro said, holding it a little gingerly. 'What is it?'

'It's a hotel,' Matthew announced. 'Like the one you and Mummy are building together.'

Scarlett looked at her son in surprise. 'How did you know about that?' she asked.

'Roxanne told me,' he said. 'She said it was the biggest con…con-something you had ever done.'

'Contract,' she said. 'It's like an agreement or a promise, but it's written on paper and both people sign it.'

'When I grow up I want to have lots of hotels too,' Matthew said. 'And lots of cars, just like *Papa* does.'

Alessandro felt a knife-like pain rise in his chest. What if his son didn't get the chance to grow up? Like Marco, he might not even get to see the day he came of age. He couldn't believe how much it hurt him to even think about the possibility of losing his little son. He had only known him a few days, and yet the love he felt for him was as strong as any devoted father's, he was sure. It filled him, it consumed every waking moment—the need to protect his flesh and blood in every way possible.

He forced a smile to his face and bent down to be on a level with Matthew. 'We have come early because we have something special to tell you.'

Matthew's eyes became bug-like with excitement. 'Am I getting a puppy?' He started to jump up and down. 'Am I? *Am I?*'

'No, darling,' Scarlett said. 'It's not a puppy.'

Alessandro watched as his son's little shoulders slumped, Matthew's bottom lip trying not to pout in disappointment but failing. 'We will think about a puppy,' he found himself saying as he laid a hand on Matthew's little bony shoulder.

'Really?' Matthew asked, eyes wide with anticipation.

Alessandro gave the little shoulder under his large hand a gentle squeeze. 'Of course we will. You can even choose its name.'

Scarlett sent Alessandro a cautionary glance but he ignored it as he continued, 'Matthew, your mother and I are getting married in a few days. That means basically that you will not be living in the flat alone with your mother but with me at my house.'

Matthew's little face fell, his hazel eyes wide with worry. 'Is…is Mummy going to be there too?' he asked.

Alessandro frowned. 'Of course she is. That is what being married means. Two people living together.'

Matthew worked at his bottom lip for a moment before releasing it. 'But Ben's parents are married, but his mummy lives with someone else now.'

Alessandro looked at Scarlett for help. 'Can you explain this? I do not seem to be doing such a great job of it,' he said with a rueful grimace.

Scarlett ruffled her son's hair and smiled at him tenderly. 'Ben's mum and dad are going through a divorce, which means they don't want to live together any more. Your father and I, er, do want to live together so we can both be with you all the time.'

'So I will always have a live daddy now?' Matthew asked.

'Yes,' Alessandro said, his throat feeling tight. 'I will always be there for you. Now, run along and get your things as we are going out tonight to celebrate becoming a family.'

Scarlett had to wait until Matthew was out of earshot. 'I

don't think you should have said you were going to be with him indefinitely.'

He looked down at her. 'Why not?'

She hoisted the strap of her bag back over her shoulder and checked to see where Matthew was before she answered. 'You intimated to me that our marriage was going to be temporary.'

'It will last as long as it needs to last to provide for my son. I want him to visit my country. I want him to learn my language.'

She threw him another reproachful look. 'Promising him a puppy was totally out of line. Dogs need a lot of care and attention, and unless they spend inordinately long periods of time in quarantine they cannot travel overseas.'

'I want to give him what he wants—surely that is my privilege as his father?'

'You're trying too hard,' she said, conscious of Matthew scampering over towards them with his little backpack slung over one shoulder.

'Do not tell me how to be a father to him,' Alessandro said in a harsh undertone. 'You are his mother, you know nothing of what being a father involves.'

Scarlett gave him a stringent look. 'I have been both mother and father to him for the last three years, so don't tell me what I do and do not know.'

Grey-blue eyes warred with hazel, but in the end it was Matthew who broke the gridlock. 'Where are we going to celebrate being a family?' he asked.

Alessandro took his son's little hand in his. 'Where would *you* like to go?' he asked.

'I just want to be where you and Mummy are,' he said with an engaging smile. 'But somewhere where there is chips would be good. I love them, but Mummy won't always let me have them.'

'That's because I want you to be as healthy as you can possibly be, darling,' Scarlett said. 'I want you to grow up big and strong.'

'Just like *Papa*?' Matthew asked, doing a little skip as he held tightly to his father's hand.

Scarlett saw the up-and-down movement of Alessandro's throat and the shadow of grief come and go in his eyes as they briefly met hers. 'Yes,' she said softly. 'Just like *Papa*.'

'Is he asleep?' Scarlett asked, peering around Matthew's bedroom door later that evening after she had seen the doctor out.

Alessandro stood up, his sudden increase in height making the room seem even smaller than it was. 'Yes,' he said, closing the book he had been reading. 'He fell asleep on the first page, but I kept reading.'

Scarlett looked at the title and inwardly frowned. 'That's probably a bit advanced for him,' she said, indicating the copy of C. S. Lewis's *The Lion, the Witch and the Wardrobe* in his hand.

He turned away from her to place it back on the small shelf amongst the picture books and children's Bible. 'I know, but my brother really loved it when he was a child. I used to read it to him when he was in hospital for long periods. I just thought…'

She took a step towards him even before she realised she'd moved. 'Alessandro…'

He turned back to face her, his expression frighteningly grave. 'We need to talk.'

'Yes—yes, I know.'

He led her out of the room, reaching for the light switch at the same time she did, his hand coming over hers.

Scarlett met his gaze in the semi-darkness, her heart feeling as if it was going to burst from her chest as his long warm fingers curled around hers.

She didn't pull away when he took her hand in his and led her through to the small sitting-room, where he took the sofa opposite once she was seated.

'The DNA test will tell us if he is a carrier or likely to develop the disease,' he said into the silence. 'We need to prepare ourselves for the results.'

Scarlett could feel the hammer of dread she had been trying to ignore begin to pound again deep inside her, the shock-waves reverberating with terrifying, sickening clamour inside her head.

She couldn't bear the thought of her precious little boy becoming ill in any shape or form, much less with a disease with no known cure at this point in time. The thought of Matthew being a carrier was perhaps a little less distressing, although she imagined it would be a heavy burden for him to carry when he became an adult and started thinking about having children of his own.

Alessandro sent his hand through the thickness of his glossy black hair and met her gaze once more. 'I have so many regrets about how I have handled this situation,' he said. 'I realise there is very little possibility of you ever forgiving me for letting you down the way I did, but I beg that you will try and find in it in yourself to do so.'

There was a beat or two of silence.

'I do forgive you, Alessandro,' she said, surprised that she actually meant it.

His eyes contained a hint of moisture, and his throat looked as if he was having trouble swallowing. 'I do not deserve such ready forgiveness, Scarlett,' he said. 'You should be making me suffer much more for my sins.'

She gave him a twisted smile. 'I think there has been suffering enough on both sides without any more being added to the pile. Matthew is the important one now. We have to concentrate on what his needs are now and in the future.'

'Yes,' he said, sighing as he looked down at his hands for a moment before raising his gaze again. 'Whatever happens…' he paused as he fought for control. 'I want to thank you for having him. It is an experience I had so very determinedly decided I would never have—and yet seeing him living and breathing, laughing and smiling, has made me realise my life would have missed something very precious if fate had not stepped in the way it did.'

'You believe it was fate?' she asked.

He gave her a glimmer of a smile. 'Meeting you that day in Milan was fate, was it not?' he asked. 'Remember?'

Scarlett remembered it all too well—the way she had tripped over something on the pavement and had pitched headlong into Alessandro's tall body coming the other way, her face practically buried in his groin until she had righted herself with the help of his strong hands on her upper arms.

The instant jolt of attraction had taken her completely by surprise. Her heart had felt as if it had been short-circuited by the electricity charging from his body to hers where he'd been still holding her. She had smiled up at him in embarrassment, her stomach doing somersaults and backflips when he'd smiled back.

'Yes…' she said, moistening her mouth. 'I remember.'

'The ceremony will be a simple one at five in the afternoon,' he said after a short pause.

'I see,' she said, not sure there was anything else she could say to stop the fast-moving train of Alessandro's determination.

Things were rapidly moving out of her control, and yet she could barely get her voice to frame a protest. It seemed Alessandro was intent on getting things done, and done quickly, and nothing and no one was going to stand in his way. It worried her that she was so willingly going along with everything, but she couldn't find it in herself to try and stop the process of her life being totally subsumed into his. He was trying to make up for lost time, and yet he had not once mentioned his feelings for her. He cared for Matthew, that much was clear, why else would he have insisted on giving him the protection of his name?

As to what he felt for her, that remained a mystery. He desired her, but then physical attraction was always so much less complicated for men than for women. It had been that way in their relationship four years ago. She had fallen in love with him but he had not once voiced the reciprocation of those feelings.

'I have also organised an appointment with a dress designer, as well as a hair and make-up session. I will take care of Matthew while you are otherwise occupied.'

'You seem to have thought of everything…' she said with a little frown. 'But what about my flat and all my things? I still have six months on my lease.'

'The lease I will take care of,' he said and, rising to his feet, gave the sitting room a cursory glance before he added, 'But there does not seem to be very much to move. My staff will see to it during the ceremony so as not to disturb you or Matthew.'

'What about guests?' she asked. 'Am I allowed to invite anyone?'

'If you would like to do so, then of course, but I would like to keep things fairly low-key and simple. We will not have a full reception, just some champagne and hors d'oeuvres before we settle in as a family at my house.'

She gave him a look that contained a hint of petulance. 'There doesn't seem much for me to do except turn up at the church on time.'

'I have tried to make things easier for you by taking care of every detail, Scarlett,' he said with an element of frustration in his tone. 'It would be unfair to expect you to organise a wedding at short notice on top of your work commitments.'

'You are controlling everything as if I'm a puppet that has to dance when you say so,' she said as she rose from the sofa in one jerky movement. 'What about what I want? Have you thought about that?'

He drew in a breath and came to stand in front of her. 'I know that you want what is best for Matthew,' he said. 'That has been your number-one priority thus far, has it not?'

She pressed her lips together and lowering her eyes, she nodded. 'Yes. Yes, of course it has.'

He tipped up her chin and locked gazes with her. 'Then on that we are united, *cara*,' he said. 'Is that not a good place on which to start a marriage?'

'I just wish…' She gnawed at her bottom lip momentarily. 'I just wish things were different…you know…between us.'

Scarlett felt him tug her towards him. It was such a gentle movement, but she could feel the steely purpose underpinning it. She went all too willingly, her body coming into contact with his from chest to thigh. She moistened her mouth again, her eyes going to the sensual curve of his, her body set alight by the embers smouldering in his hazel gaze as it secured hers.

'I want you like I have wanted no other woman,' he said, skimming his hands down to her cup her breasts, and shaping her intimately until she began to whimper in response. 'I want you now. I told myself I would wait until we are officially married, but I cannot stop this urge to have you in my arms again. I have been fighting it all day.'

'I've been fighting it too,' she confessed. 'I thought I hated you but…..but I…..but I don't….'

His hands stilled on her. 'I do not want your pity,' he said, frowning. 'You do not have to sleep with me because you feel sorry for me.'

'It's not about that,' she said in earnest. 'I want you just as much as you seem to want me, maybe even more so.'

His hands gently cupped her face. 'I cannot give you what you want, Scarlett. I cannot give you what you deserve. You spoke of your longing for another child. You must realise I cannot agree to that.'

'But I'm not a carrier,' she said. 'Matthew is fine. I just know he is.' *I am praying he is,* she inserted silently. 'We could have another baby, another two babies, and they could be just as healthy as he is.'

His hands fell away from her face. 'No. I will not allow a child of mine to suffer the way Marco did.'

'I'll have a test! Then you'll see it's OK.'

'You are forgetting something, Scarlett,' he said heavily. 'It is not a matter of playing Russian roulette. I am a carrier, Matthew could be too, and so too could any other child I father. I had genetic counselling years ago. There is a fifty-percent chance of me fathering a child who is a carrier. I do not want that on my conscience.'

She looked at him in despair. 'But…but I could already be pregnant.'

He brought her chin up so she had to meet his gaze. 'We will deal with it,' he said. 'We will deal with it if it turns out you are pregnant.'

She swallowed back the painful restriction in her throat. 'You're not asking me to…to…'

He shook his head. 'No, of course not. That is your decision and one I will support either way.'

'I can't do it, Alessandro,' she inserted passionately. 'My father asked it of my mother, and she wouldn't do it. I wouldn't be here today if she had done what he had insisted.'

He cupped her face once more, his eyes warm as they held hers. 'I would not ask that of you. You were very brave to have gone ahead with the pregnancy with Matthew. You had no one to support you, but if you are pregnant this time I will stand by you. But in the meantime all I am asking of you is to give me a chance to be a father to my son.'

'I w-won't stand in your way,' she said, emotion contorting her voice. 'I want you to be there for him. I really do.'

'So you will agree to marry me next Friday?'

'I can't believe I'm saying this, but yes, I will marry you.'

'I hope you will not regret doing so, Scarlett,' he said. 'I will make sure you are well provided for if things do not work out.'

'You mean…if…I mean when we get divorced?'

'If anything should happen to Matthew…' He swallowed tightly and continued. 'I would not want you to be tied to me, as my mother has been to my father, in a loveless, pointless marriage.'

She looked up into Alessandro's tortured face and felt the last, hard nut of her anger dissolve completely. 'You love him, don't you? You love Matthew even though you've only known him such a short time.'

He put his hand to the nape of her neck and pulled her back against his chest. 'Yes,' he said on the tail end of a deep sigh. 'I did not think it was possible, as I have not allowed myself to feel anything more than mild affection for anyone for many years.'

She lifted her head and met his hazel gaze. 'Is that what you felt for me four years ago—mild affection?'

A small frown began to pull at Alessandro's brows as he looked down at her. 'No,' he said. 'What I felt for you was different.'

She ran her tongue over her lips in an apprehensive gesture, her gaze still locked on his. 'Are you going to tell me?' she asked.

He lifted her off her feet and carried her to her bedroom next door. 'I would much rather show you,' he said, and kicked the door shut with his foot.

CHAPTER THIRTEEN

SCARLETT WOKE during the early hours of the morning to find one of Alessandro's hair-roughened thighs lying heavily over one of her smoother ones, and her breasts pressed against the possessive band of his arm. Her bottom was wedged against his pelvis, the hard ridge of his erection nudging her provocatively from behind.

She wriggled experimentally, and his mouth began to nuzzle against her neck. 'You are not tired of me yet, *cara*?' he asked in smouldering tones.

Scarlett knew she would never be tired of him. He made her whole body pulse and hum with erotic delight, and even though they had made love twice earlier she felt her need for him building all over again. 'I thought you were asleep,' she said, too shy to admit how much she wanted him.

He turned her over, his body pressing its delicious temptation against hers. 'I was, but I was dreaming of you,' he said. 'I have done that a lot just lately.'

Hope lifted like a balloon in her chest. 'Have you?'

He smiled and pressed a teasing kiss to the side of her mouth, so close to, but not quite touching, her lips that tingled for his touch. 'Not just lately,' he confessed. 'For years, actually. I have never forgotten how you felt in my arms.'

Scarlett felt her love for him rising to the surface of her skin like champagne bubbles spilling over the rim of a glass. She was overflowing with love for him. Every pore of her body was soaked with it. She touched his face, her soft fingers catching on the stubble that had grown along his jawline in the hours they had been in bed, her stomach doing a little fluttery movement as he reached past her for where his wallet was lying on the bedside table.

'I have only one condom left,' he said as he tore open the packet with his teeth. 'That is, unless you have a supply handy.'

A tiny frown pulled at her forehead. 'I told you, Alessandro, I haven't slept with anyone since you. Don't you believe me?'

It seemed a long time before he answered. 'Yes, I believe you.'

She looked at him, her stomach tripping over itself at the look of respect she could see in his eyes as they held hers.

'You have been a wonderful mother to my son,' he said in a husky tone. 'I know I have said it before, but I do not know how to thank you for protecting him the way you have done. You have sacrificed your own life to provide for him.'

'I love him, Alessandro,' she said softly. 'As soon as I knew I was carrying him I loved him.' *And I love you too*, she desperately wanted to add, but she realised he wasn't quite ready to hear it.

So much had happened in such a short time. He was struggling with a host of complex emotions—regret, guilt and grief at what he had lost so far in his little son's life. She could see the pain in his eyes; it was etched too in every chiselled feature on his face. She would only be adding to his burden of guilt to tell him she had never stopped loving him.

Besides, he might not believe her. He might think she was only saying it out of pity, as he had hinted at earlier. He was a private man, but a very proud one for all that. There would hopefully be time after they were married and Matthew's health status was established.

She reached up and stroked his face again, his gaze burning with sensual promise as it held hers.

'I cannot wait much longer,' he said, his now-sheathed body searching for the silken warmth of hers. 'I do not want to make you sore, but I cannot quench my desire for you.'

'I'll be fine,' she said, opening her legs to accommodate him, sighing in bliss when he surged into her heated core. 'It feels as if you have never been away.'

He kissed her deeply, his tongue setting fire to hers as his body rocked against her in the passionate climb to the summit of sensual release. Scarlett was with him every step of the way, her body tensing exquisitely, inexorably, as he brought her breathlessly to that final moment of suspension between agony and ecstasy.

She finally tipped over with a high cry of pleasure that came from deep within her body, the waves rolling her over and over until she was lying totally spent in his arms. Her breathing was still choppy and uneven as she felt him pump himself to paradise, his harsh groan of release making her skin lift in a shiver of delight that she had brought him to this moment.

She stroked his back with her fingers, up and down in slow, sweeping, caressing movements that brought another sigh of deep pleasure from his throat. 'You have such a sensual touch,' he said against her neck, the movement of his lips tickling her sensitive skin.

'I'm a little out of practice,' she said, becoming bolder as she stroked the taut curve of his buttocks.

He propped himself up on his elbows to look down at her. 'I am sure we will get you back up to scratch in no time at all.'

She toyed with a strand of his hair that persisted in falling forward. 'How long do you think our marriage will last?' she asked, not quite able to meet his eyes.

He frowned, and captured her hand to still its movements. 'I cannot really answer that,' he said. 'No one can answer that these days. It is up to so many variables.'

'It's a big commitment,' she said, bringing her eyes back to his. 'And a legally binding one.'

A glint of cynicism entered his gaze. 'I have already told you that you will be well provided for if or when we decide to bring the marriage to an end.'

'I wasn't suggesting—'

'Before we marry there are legal papers to sign,' he said. 'I have to protect my business interests and my shareholders. I do not mean any offence, but that is the way it has to be. Prenuptial agreements are more or less commonplace these days.'

'Not between couples who trust each other,' she said. 'You seem to be suggesting that I will take the first opportunity I can to grab half of your assets.'

'You have every motivation to do so, Scarlett,' he reminded her. 'What better revenge than to have me lulled into a false sense of security? I have let you down—not intentionally, of course, but no less despicably, and dare I say unforgivably. Even though you say you have forgiven me, you could very well be quietly plotting and planning your revenge—but I am not going to allow it to come to fruition for one reason and one reason only.'

'Let me guess,' she said with a scornful glare as she tried ineffectually to get out from under the erotic weight of his body entrapping hers. 'Your pride is the issue at stake here. That's all you really care about it, isn't it? Your damned pride.'

'No,' he said, capturing her flailing hands and holding them above her head. 'This is not about my pride. It is about our son. He does not deserve to be exposed to whatever bitterness we feel towards each other.'

Scarlett felt tipped off course emotionally as she struggled against his hold. *She* was the one who was supposed to be feeling bitter, not him. What did he have to feel bitter about? It wasn't as if she had kept their child a secret from him. She had been upfront and honest from the word go, but *he* had chosen not to believe her. 'Let me go,' she bit out, arching and bucking beneath him.

His green-brown eyes glinted as her body came into intimate contact with his. 'You do not really mean that, Scarlett, now do you?'

She arched her spine again, but it only intensified the intimacy. She couldn't resist him now. She gasped in submission as he slid inside her needy warmth, her body wrapping around him tightly, almost greedily.

'No, you don't,' he said, sweeping his tongue over the trembling bow of her lips. 'You want me even though you hate me, but I do not care. I would rather have you hating me than not have you at all.'

I don't hate you, Scarlett mentally chanted as his mouth came down like a burst of flame upon hers.

* * *

'You're getting *married* to him?' Roxanne asked incredulously. 'Wow, that man sure can sure charm the birds from the bees.'

'Trees,' Scarlett said, mentally rolling her eyes.

'Have you told your mum?' Roxanne asked.

'I called her this morning after Alessandro left.'

'And?'

'And she's happy for me.'

'Are you happy for you?' Roxanne asked with a penetrating look.

Scarlett let out a little sigh. 'I'm so frightened for Matthew. We both are. We have to wait a few days for the test results. I feel like an axe is hanging over our heads. It could drop at any moment.'

'But he might not have it,' Roxanne said, echoing what Scarlett's mother had said earlier. 'You might be worrying for nothing.'

Scarlett looked at the screen saver and wondered how many years of photographs she would have of her son if it turned out he was a sufferer. 'I just can't imagine what life would be like without him,' she said, biting her lip.

Roxanne bent down and gave her a big hug. 'You're not going to lose him, Scarlett,' she said. 'Don't even think about it.'

Scarlett was working on some of the layouts for the Marciano Palazzo Hotel when Alessandro arrived with his lawyer. She forced a smile to her lips as she greeted the older man, who after exchanging a few cursory words placed the papers in front of her to sign.

She picked up a pen and, sending Alessandro a brittle little glare, bent her head to the documents, reading through each one with studious deliberation. She was conscious of the minutes ticking by as she turned each page, but finally she came to the end and signed the highlighted spaces.

Once the lawyer had left Alessandro turned to Scarlett. 'Do you have time for a coffee, *cara*?' he asked.

Scarlett considered refusing, but Roxanne was within earshot. 'All right,' she said, removing her glasses. 'But I haven't got long.'

'You are not working too hard, are you?' he asked as he held the door open for her.

'It's what I'm being paid to do, isn't it?' she returned.

He took her elbow as he led her across to where his car was parked. 'The hotel refurbishment is not high on my list of priorities right now,' he said heavily. 'All I can think about is Matthew.'

Scarlett felt her defenses take a tumble. 'Me too,' she said, glancing up at him, her expression full of fear.

He gave her elbow a gentle squeeze, his eyes softening as they met hers. 'We will not know anything for at least a week. I know it is hard, but at least we have the wedding to distract us.'

They sat in a café a short time later with steaming coffees in front of them. Scarlett poked at the foam on hers with a teaspoon, her brow still wrinkled with worry.

'Here is the number of the dress designer.' He handed her a card across the table. 'She will fit you with whatever you need for the day at my expense.'

Scarlett looked down at the bridal designer's name on the card before returning her surprised gaze to his. 'You want me to be a real bride?' she asked.

'But of course,' he said. 'Is that not every young woman's dream?'

She pressed her lips together as she tucked the card into

her purse. 'I was expecting a quick civil service,' she said. 'I'm surprised you want to go to so much trouble, especially given the limited time.'

'I am trying to right the wrongs of the past,' he said. 'You said you wanted marriage and babies. I cannot agree to another child, but the least I can do is give you a wedding day to remember.'

Scarlett concentrated on pushing at the foam on her coffee again rather than meet his eyes.

'I am going to have the surgery redone tomorrow,' he said after a protracted silence.

She looked up at him again. 'Would you like me to come with you?'

'That will not be necessary,' he said. 'It is a simple procedure.'

'But it still requires a general anaesthetic, right?'

He gave her a lopsided smile. 'Do not concern yourself with my welfare, Scarlett. I know you would prefer it if I met with a dastardly end, but as you see I am in excellent health.'

She frowned at his tone. 'I don't wish any such thing on you or anyone,' she said. 'I just thought you might like some support. It's scary going into hospital on your own.'

'Are you offering to accompany me just to make me feel even guiltier about the support I refused to give you four years ago?' he asked with a flinty look.

'No, of course not,' she said, still frowning.

He shifted his gaze and pushed his barely touched coffee away. 'I am suffering enough as it is without you heaping burning coals upon my head.'

Scarlett felt tears burning at the back of her throat. 'I know,' she said. 'I'm sorry.'

He reached for her hand and brought it up to his mouth,

kissing it softly as his eyes met hers. 'I am being a brute, *tesore mio*,' he said in a gruff tone. 'It must be pre-wedding jitters, no?'

She tried to smile but couldn't quite pull it off. 'We're both on edge,' she said, suppressing a tiny shiver as his lips pressed against her fingertips once more. 'We both stand to lose the one person we love more than any other.'

His fingers tightened momentarily around hers. 'We are not going to lose him, *cara*,' he said. 'Not if I can help it.'

CHAPTER FOURTEEN

'ARE YOU sure about this?' Scarlett asked Roxanne the following evening. 'I mean, Alessandro's not really expecting me to drop in, so if you want to cancel…'

'Stop fussing, Scarlett,' Roxanne said. 'Besides, I think it would be a nice gesture to turn up with some flowers. Alessandro would be feeling pretty sore and sorry for himself, I would imagine.'

Not that he would ever let on, Scarlett thought as she drove to Alessandro's house a few minutes later. The lights were on downstairs, which signalled he was still up, but it seemed an age before he answered the doorbell.

'Hi,' she said, thrusting the flowers forwards. 'Umm…I thought you might like these.'

He took the flowers from her after a small hesitation and, raking his fingers through his tousled hair, stepped back from the doorway. 'I wasn't expecting visitors.'

'I know, but I just thought…' She shuffled from foot to foot. 'You know…that you might not want to be alone right now.'

She heard him pull in a breath as he put the flowers to one side, the sound of the cellophane wrapping as it crinkled under his fingers sounding like gunshots in the silence.

'How are you feeling?' she asked.

He turned to face her. 'I am fine. A bit sleepy, but that is to be expected.'

There was another short silence.

'Have you eaten?' she asked.

'I am not hungry.'

'I could make you something,' she offered. 'An omelette or a boiled egg, or—'

'Why are you here?'

Scarlett flinched at his sharp tone. 'I'm here because you shouldn't be alone right now.'

'What if I want to be alone right now?'

She waited for two or three seconds to ask, 'Do you want me to leave?'

He held her gaze for a moment before turning away to stare at the flowers she had brought. 'That was my mistake four years ago,' he said. 'I should never have sent you away. I should have checked and double checked before I did that.'

'You weren't to know,' she said in a creaky voice. 'You didn't do it on purpose, it was just the way things turned out.'

He swung around to look at her. 'How can you stand there and be so damned charitable about this?'

She moistened her paper-dry lips. 'Because you are my son's father.'

He sucked in a harsh breath and swung away again. 'But what sort of father am I?' he rasped. 'I have given him a legacy that is going to be with him and his offspring for God knows how many generations.'

'I don't see it that way,' she said. 'You can give him so much. And I don't mean in terms of money. You have so much that is good in you, Alessandro. You are a wonderful person. You could have turned your back on him, but you didn't once you knew for sure he was yours. He loves you. He told me so this evening when I tucked him into bed before Roxanne came around to babysit. He *loves* you.'

She saw his knuckles whiten where he was gripping the small marble table where he had laid the flowers down. 'I should not have doubted you, Scarlett,' he said. 'I have robbed myself of the first three years of my son's life. How can I ever repair that damage?'

'Children are not like adults,' she said, fighting back tears. 'They don't hold grudges and they don't judge. I am sure by the time Matthew is of school age he will not even remember that you weren't there for the first three years of his life. You are his father now—that is all that matters.'

He turned back to face her, his expression so tortured she felt an answering pain deep inside her chest. 'I want to be a father to him,' he said in a tone raw and deep with emotion. 'I want to do the things with him that my father could not do because of Marco's illness.'

'You will do that, and more,' she said softly. 'I know you will.'

He let out a sigh and took the three steps that separated them, his arms enfolding her into his rock-hard embrace. 'I do not understand how you can be so gracious. I would not be the same in your place. I would never have been able to forgive what you have forgiven. You are a much better person than me.'

'That is not true,' she said. 'I haven't had to face the issues you've had to face.'

'But you have to face them now.'

'I know, but I still don't think Matthew's—'

He put her from him abruptly. 'Wishing and hoping does not cut it I am afraid, Scarlett,' he said. 'Do you not think my parents did not do the very same? They prayed and wished and hoped and begged, but it did nothing to change what happened in the end.'

'I know. It's just I want to keep positive for as long as I can for Matthew's sake.'

He let out a sigh and sent his hand through his hair again. 'Go home, Scarlett,' he said. 'You do not have to be a devoted wife until Friday. These are your last days of freedom—do not waste them on me.'

Scarlett reached up on tiptoe and pressed a kiss to his cheek. 'I hope you're feeling better soon,' she said softly.

He brushed the side of her face with the back of his knuckles in a caress so gentle she felt tears start to well in her eyes. 'I will see you in church,' he said. 'I have to go back to Melbourne for a couple of days. If there is anything you need in the meantime, do not hesitate to call me.'

She moistened her lips and stepped back to leave, but he caught her arm and brought her up close, his mouth pressing down on hers in a brief but possessive kiss that sent flames of need to every sensual spot in her body.

It was over as quickly as it began.

She stood blinking up at him when he released her, her heart going like a misfiring engine, and her stomach coiling with need.

'Go home, Scarlett,' he repeated.

Scarlett let out a shaky sigh and left.

The day of the wedding arrived with brilliant sunshine and humid heat, but Scarlett barely noticed as she and Matthew arrived at the cathedral in the car Alessandro had sent for them.

Clutching the bouquet of fragrant gardenias he'd had delivered to her flat that morning, Scarlett gave her little son a smile as they walked past the flashing cameras of the press to where Alessandro was waiting at the end of the aisle for them both.

The vows were exchanged before the public kiss that seemed to Scarlett to contain such a private promise of passion.

She looked into Alessandro's eyes as he lifted his mouth from hers and felt her belly quiver with anticipation. She could see the desire shining in his eyes, and her heart began to clip-clop erratically at the thought of being his wife in every sense of the word.

'Mummy?'

Scarlett was jerked out of her eye-lock with Alessandro to the little figure standing between them. 'Yes, darling?'

'Are we a family now?' Matthew asked, his stage whisper echoing throughout the cavernous cathedral.

She felt her heart contract when Alessandro bent down and lifted him into his arms. 'Yes, Matthew,' he said, the mist of emotion unmistakable in the hazel depths of his eyes as they met hers. 'We are a proper family now.'

After Scarlett had introduced Alessandro to her mother and sister there was barely time for photographs before he said it was time to leave. She could sense his impatience to get away from the persistent press, but she realised it was because he was trying to protect Matthew more than anything else.

Matthew chattered non-stop in the car on the journey back to Alessandro's house, which relieved Scarlett of the task of thinking of something to say. She still found it hard to believe she was now legally married to him. Four years ago she would have given anything to have his ring on her finger and yet, looking down at the simple white-gold band now, she couldn't help wondering how long it was going to stay there.

'You are savaging that lip of yours again, *cara*,' Alessandro said as he carried a now fast-asleep Matthew into the house a short time later. 'Do I make you so nervous?'

She let her lip go, feeling a blush steal into her cheeks. 'No… It's just that it's a big change, you know, being married instead of single.'

'I enjoyed meeting your mother,' he said as he handed her the keys to unlock the front door. 'She reminds me of you.'

Scarlett concentrated on fitting the key into the lock. 'Yes, we're very alike,' she said, thinking of how hurt her mother had been by her father. She only hoped history wasn't going to repeat itself in her life with Alessandro.

Matthew opened his eyes and blinked a couple of times. *'Papa?* Is this your house?' he asked looking around the huge foyer with wonder.

'Yes, my son, it is,' Alessandro answered. 'But now it is also yours and your mother's home too.'

Scarlett turned away from his glinting look to address her son. 'Matthew, it's time you were in bed. It's been a long day.'

'But I'm not tired,' Matthew protested. 'And I want to look around my new house.'

'You can do that tomorrow, but for now—'

'I will show you around for a few minutes before I tuck you in,' Alessandro said to Matthew. 'You should at least know where everything is the first night in a new place.'

Scarlett glared at him silently.

'Your things have been placed in my room,' he said to her with an inscrutable expression on his face. 'Matthew will be in the room closest to ours. My housekeeper has already unpacked everything, so you will be able to get changed.'

She turned away without responding, her arms going across her body in an attempt to control her emotions. She felt like she was already losing her son. Alessandro was taking command of everything, leaving her with no authority where Matthew was concerned. She could see how within weeks she would have no place in her son's life. She would be shunted to one side while Alessandro took control, indulging Matthew, giving him the things she had never been able to afford to provide.

'Mummy, are you going to come up and kiss me good-night?' Matthew asked a few minutes later as he and Alessandro returned from a tour of the lower floor and garden.

Scarlett met Alessandro's gaze with an arch look. 'Am I allowed to?' she asked.

His brows moved together slightly. 'He is your son as well as mine, Scarlett,' he said. 'You do not have to change your routines with him on account of me.'

'Don't I?'

His frown deepened. 'We will talk about this later. Come, Matthew, we will do your teeth and get you into your pyjamas so that Mummy can tuck you in.'

'But I want *you* to tuck me in,' Matthew said with a little pout. 'Mummy's done it heaps of times, but I want you to do it now.'

Scarlett gave Alessandro a 'see what you've done now?' glare.

He held her look for a tense moment before addressing Matthew with quiet authority. 'We will both tuck you in on the nights we are here together.'

Matthew's little brow wrinkled. 'But aren't you going to be here every night from now on?' he asked.

'I sometimes have to travel,' Alessandro said after a small

pause. 'I also sometimes have to work long hours, but I will try to be here as much as possible.'

'I don't want you to go away without me,' Matthew said, and with a beseeching look added, 'Can't Mummy and I come with you everywhere you go?'

'That might not always be possible, Matthew,' he said, briefly meeting Scarlett's gaze. 'I have a business to run in Italy, and your mother has her business to see to here.'

'I know! Mummy can sell her business to Roxanne, and then we can be with you all the time,' Matthew said, clearly proud of his solution.

'We will see about that,' Alessandro said with another in-scrutable look at Scarlett, and led the way upstairs.

Scarlett had barely closed the door on her son's sleeping figure a few minutes later when she rounded on Alessandro. 'How dare you override my authority like that?'

He fixed her with a level stare. 'Keep your voice down,' he commanded quietly.

She glared at him, her hands in fists at her sides. 'Don't tell me what to do. If I want to shout at you, I will shout.'

His eyes became hard as they clashed with hers. 'You will not raise your voice to me, and certainly not within the hearing distance of Matthew,' he said, still in the same quiet but steely tone.

Scarlett brushed past him to stomp into the master bedroom where she proceeded to remove her things from the walk-in wardrobe in a haphazard fashion.

'What do you think you are doing?' he asked.

She spun around to face him, her arms full of clothes. 'I'm not going to share a room with you,' she said. 'I'm not going to share anything with you. I wish I'd never married you.'

'Put the clothes down, Scarlett,' he commanded.

Tears shone in her eyes. 'You're going to take him away from me, aren't you?' she asked, holding the clothes like a shield against her. 'That's your plan, isn't it?'

'You are talking rubbish, Scarlett. I have no such plan.'

'I don't believe you,' she said, struggling not to cry. 'As soon as you realised he is yours, you've been systematically eroding my place in his life so when we divorce he'll want to live with you instead of me.'

'That is not true.'

'I won't let you do it, Alessandro,' she said. 'I won't let you turn him against me.'

He let out a breath and came towards her. '*Cara*, the last thing I want to do is take him away from you. You are his mother.'

'But you said our marriage was temporary.'

'I have said a lot of things I am deeply ashamed of saying,' he said. 'But how else was I to get you to do what I wanted you to do?'

She swallowed as some of the clothes in her grasp slipped to the floor. 'I'm not sure what you're saying…'

'I am saying that the only way I could see to get you to agree to marry me was to leave you no choice in the matter,' he said. 'I let you down four years ago. I turned my back on you and our son out of sheer ignorance and arrogance. I will never forgive myself for that. Every time I see that photograph of you standing outside that hospital with him in your arms, I feel like a saw is tearing at my insides.'

'You…you do?'

He nodded as he removed the rest of the clothes from her arms and laid them to one side. 'I should have been there for you, *cara*. I cannot get that time back no matter how much I want to. If it had not been for my medical history, I would have asked you to marry me four years ago.'

Her eyes went wide. 'You…you would?'

He touched her bottom lip with his thumb. 'I had only realised a couple of days before you told me you were pregnant that I was in love with you. I was fighting it for weeks, as I knew it would bring up the difficult issue of children. You were so young to give up that dream. I did not think I could ask it of you.'

'I would have given it up for you,' she said softly. 'I would have done anything to have stayed with you.'

His thumbs blotted the steady pathway of tears making their way down her cheeks. 'But it was already too late,' he said. 'You were carrying my son.'

She choked back a little sob. 'Yes.'

'I love you, Scarlett,' he said. 'I think perhaps I always did, even when I thought you had lied to me. That is why I reacted the way I did. If I had not cared for you, I would not have felt so betrayed.'

She looked at him in amazement. 'You still *love* me?'

'Yes, *cara*, I do. But it has taken me a long time to realise it.'

'Alessandro, I am so happy, but so frightened at the same time,' she confessed. 'I thought I'd lost you for ever, and now I have you, but Matthew could be…' She bit her lip and blinked back fresh tears.

His eyes were shadowed with pain as they held hers. 'We will have the results of the test in a day or two,' he said. 'I do not know how to prepare Matthew if it turns out he is affected or is a carrier. Either way, I feel as if I have let him down all over again.'

Scarlett grasped at his hands and squeezed them tightly.

'You mustn't think like that,' she said. 'I love you, Alessandro. Matthew does too. Whatever the test shows is not going to change that.'

His eyes misted slightly. 'I do not deserve your love,' he said. 'I think I found it easier when you said you hated me. That at least I deserved.'

'I can't hate you any more,' she said, wrapping her arms around him. 'I've tried to, but I can't. I loved you from the moment I tripped and fell into your arms.'

He brought her closer, his chin going to the top of her head. 'I wish I could protect you from whatever the future holds,' he said. 'I loved my brother *so* much. Losing him was like losing a part of myself. I have felt empty ever since.

'It was not until I met Matthew that I realised how locked down I was emotionally. But when I was reading to Matthew the other night I recalled a conversation I had with Marco not long before he died. I think he knew he did not have long. He told me how much he had enjoyed the life he had had. At the time, I could not understand why or how he would say such a thing. From my perspective he had endured nothing but constant suffering, but he did not seem to see it that way. He said he had learned so much about the value of relationships, how the love and care he had received had made him a stronger person even though he was weak physically.'

'He must have been a very brave and special person,' Scarlett said softly.

Alessandro nodded sadly. 'Indeed he was, and he would have been delighted to have been Matthew's uncle. I *want* Matthew to be well, *cara*, I want it with all my being, but I do not even know at this point if our little boy has a future. That is the worst agony for me—knowing that if he doesn't it is my fault.'

Scarlett hugged him tighter. 'We will have whatever has been allotted for us, you, me and Matthew,' she said. 'There is nothing else we can do but live in love and hope.' But even as she said the words fear leaked like a thick, choking tide into her bloodstream, making her feel weighed down with the terror of the unknown.

CHAPTER FIFTEEN

SCARLETT SAT with Alessandro in the waiting room of the doctor's surgery, her fingers encased in the warmth of his. She looked down at their joined hands and felt a fluttery feeling go through her as she recalled the intimacy they had shared over the last few days as man and wife. Passion had flared as fiery as ever between them, heightened by the love they had both confessed.

She still couldn't quite believe he still loved her, and yet every time she caught him looking at her she saw it in his eyes. They were soft and warm, in spite of the shadows he did his best to hide from her.

'Not long now,' Alessandro said, giving her hand a little squeeze.

'No…' She released a jagged sigh as she returned the pressure of his fingers.

Just then the doctor came out to the waiting room. 'Mr and Mrs Marciano? Come this way please.'

Scarlett exchanged a quick, worried glance with Alessandro as he helped her to her feet before following Dr Shaftsbury to his room.

'I have some very good news for you both,' Dr Shaftsbury

announced with a smile. 'Your son does not have cystic fibrosis.'

'Is he…?' Alessandro cleared his throat and began again, 'Is he a carrier?'

The doctor smiled. 'No, he is not.'

Scarlett burst into tears as she saw her relief reflected on Alessandro's face. He clutched at her hand and held it so tightly she felt her wedding and engagement rings cut into her flesh, but she didn't even wince.

'I can't believe it,' Alessandro was saying, shaking his head. 'All this time I have dreaded passing it on…'

'Matthew is one of the lucky ones,' Allan Shaftsbury said. 'As we discussed last week, there is a fifty-percent chance of your offspring becoming a carrier. That is an issue you will have to consider if you plan to have any more children.'

'We are not planning on any more,' Alessandro said.

Scarlett shifted restlessly in her chair.

Alessandro looked at her. 'Scarlett?'

She couldn't hold his gaze.

'Is there something you should have told me before now?' he asked.

She ran her tongue over her dry lips. 'It's too early to tell, I might be late for a whole lot of reasons.'

Alessandro reached for her hand. 'How late are you?' he asked.

She lifted her eyes to his. 'A week—eight days, actually…'

Dr Shaftsbury leaned his arms on his desk. 'If it turns out you are pregnant, you can have the foetus screened and make a decision as to whether or not to continue,' he said.

'No,' Scarlett said. 'That's not an option for me. I will love the baby no matter what.'

Alessandro's thumb began stroking Scarlett's palm as he

faced the specialist. 'I agree with Scarlett, Dr Shaftsbury,' he said. 'Sometimes these things are meant to happen.'

He got to his feet and shook the doctor's hand. 'Thank you again for your help.'

'It has been a very great pleasure,' the doctor answered with another smile.

Scarlett waited until they were outside the surgery before she spoke. 'Did you mean what you said in there?' she asked. 'About the baby?'

He stood looking down at her for a long moment, his eyes so warm with love she felt her heart contract. 'I meant it, *cara*,' he said. 'If we are indeed expecting a baby then it is what is meant to be. We will love it no matter what. You have taught me that lesson, if nothing else.'

She smiled at him with love shining in her blue gaze. 'I love you, Alessandro Marciano.'

He pressed a tender kiss to her forehead. 'I love you too, *tesore mio*. No matter what the future holds.'

Eight months later

Scarlett stood silently at the door of the lounge, watching as Alessandro looked down at his tiny daughter cradled in his arms, his expression so full of wonder and joy it brought tears to her eyes.

The news that their little girl was a carrier had been accepted with great sadness, but also a sense of relief in that she was not going to suffer in the way Alessandro's brother had done. Yes, there would be issues to face in the future, but for now they would enjoy the miracle of her infancy and childhood.

Alessandro's parents Sergio and Lucia had grown a little

closer to each other as they had got to know Matthew when Scarlett and Alessandro had visited them in the summer. And the news of Scarlett's pregnancy had clearly brought them much joy, as they had seen the happiness and fulfilment on Alessandro's face each time he looked at his little family.

They were flying over for the christening in a couple of weeks, and Roxanne and Dylan had agreed to be godparents; their recent engagement was something Scarlett had seen coming for several months.

'Is she finally asleep?' Scarlett asked Alessandro as she came into the room.

Alessandro smiled as he met her gaze. 'Yes, she is, but I am not ready to put her down. It will not hurt to hold her while she sleeps, will it?'

She came to perch beside him on the sofa where he was seated, and gently caressed the black silk of his hair. 'No, of course it won't hurt her,' she said softly. 'You are her father, and she needs to get to know your touch.'

'I am her father,' Alessandro said, still looking down at the perfect features of little Mia—the name he had chosen not just because it was Italian but because it meant 'mine'. 'I never thought I would ever say those words to anyone, but now I have two beautiful children, thanks to you tripping into my arms that day in Milan and capturing my heart.'

Scarlett pressed a soft-as-air kiss to the top of his head. 'It was meant to happen, darling,' she said. 'And I for one am very glad it did.'

'Me too,' Alessandro said, reaching for her hand and giving it a loving squeeze, his hazel eyes full of adoration as he cradled his daughter protectively against the steady beat of his heart. 'Me too…'

0708/06

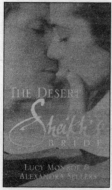

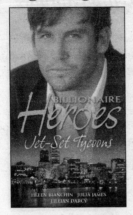 

Celebrate 100 years of pure reading pleasure with Mills & Boon®

To mark our centenary, each month we're publishing a special 100th Birthday Edition. These celebratory editions are packed with extra features and include a FREE bonus story.

Plus, you have the chance to enter a fabulous monthly prize draw. See 100th Birthday Edition books for details.

Now that's worth celebrating!

July 2008

**The Man Who Had Everything
by Christine Rimmer**
Includes FREE bonus story *Marrying Molly*

August 2008

Their Miracle Baby by Caroline Anderson
Includes FREE bonus story *Making Memories*

September 2008

Crazy About Her Spanish Boss by Rebecca Winters
Includes FREE bonus story
Rafael's Convenient Proposal

Look for Mills & Boon® 100th Birthday Editions at your favourite bookseller or visit
www.millsandboon.co.uk

4 FREE

BOOKS AND A SURPRISE GIFT!

We would like to take this opportunity to thank you for reading this Mills & Boon® book by offering you the chance to take FOUR more specially selected titles from the Modern™ series absolutely FREE! We're also making this offer to introduce you to the benefits of the Mills & Boon® Reader Service™—

- ★ **FREE home delivery**
- ★ **FREE gifts and competitions**
- ★ **FREE monthly Newsletter**
- ★ **Exclusive Reader Service offers**
- ★ **Books available before they're in the shops**

Accepting these FREE books and gift places you under no obligation to buy, you may cancel at any time, even after receiving your free shipment. Simply complete your details below and return the entire page to the address below. You don't even need a stamp!

YES! Please send me 4 free Modern books and a surprise gift. I understand that unless you hear from me, I will receive 6 superb new titles every month for just £2.99 each, postage and packing free. I am under no obligation to purchase any books and may cancel my subscription at any time. The free books and gift will be mine to keep in any case.

P8ZED

Ms/Mrs/Miss/Mr ....Initials ....

BLOCK CAPITALS PLEASE

Surname ....

Address ....

....

....Postcode..

Send this whole page to:
UK: FREEPOST CN81, Croydon, CR9 3WZ